Also by Stuart Gibbs

The Last Musketeer
The Last Musketeer: Traitor's Chase

THE LAST MUSKETEER

DOUBLE CROSS

STUART GIBBS

HARPER

An Imprint of HarperCollins*Publishers*

Library of Congress Cataloging-in-Publication Data
Gibbs, Stuart, date.
Double cross / Stuart Gibbs. — 1st ed.
    p.   cm. — (Last Musketeer ; #3)
Summary: "When Greg and the Musketeers return to Paris and
find the city under siege, they leap into action to prevent King
Louis from being overthrown and history from being changed
forever"— Provided by publisher.
ISBN 978-0-06-204844-8 (hardback)
[1. Time travel—Fiction.   2. Adventure and adventurers—
Fiction.   3. Characters in literature—Fiction.   4. Richelieu,
Armand Jean du Plessis, duc de, 1585–1642—Fiction.   5. Paris
(France)—History—17th century—Fiction.   6. France—
History—Louis XIII, 1610–1643—Fiction.]   I. Title.
PZ7.G339236Dou 2013   2012026754
[Fic]—dc23

Typography by Erin Fitzsimmons
13 14 15 16 17 LP/RRDH 10 9 8 7 6 5 4 3 2 1
❖
First Edition

For Mike Matthews, Ken Parker & Mark Middleman,
my original three Musketeers

ACKNOWLEDGMENTS

I WAS INSPIRED TO WRITE THE MEDICAL SEQUENCE IN THIS book by my father, Dr. Ronald Gibbs, who has always been fascinated by the history of surgery and medical care. His advice was of great help to me. Thanks, Dad.

I'd also like to thank Jessica Penzias, who helped me with the research for this book (and its predecessor), and Emily Mullin, who did so much great research for me on book one of this series that I was still using her notes and maps as I wrote this.

Finally, I must thank my wife, Suzanne, who pointed me toward Les Baux de Provence as the perfect place to set the beginning of this adventure—and who didn't mind me spending several hours traipsing about those ruins in the rain, trying to plot out the Musketeers' escape.

PROLOGUE

Castillon-du-Gard, France
Four hundred miles south of Paris
August 1615

EVEN THOUGH MICHEL DINICOEUR WAS IMMORTAL, HE could still feel pain. And right now, he was in agony. In the four hundred years he'd lived, he'd experienced a great deal of misery—and yet this was the worst so far.

The ordeal he'd been through would have killed a regular man. He'd been shot by flaming arrows, had fallen off a ten-story bridge, and had been swept through a raging river. His flesh was scorched and his bones were fractured. He'd swallowed enough water to drown a fish. During the past few days, he often had wished he could die and end his suffering.

Only one thing kept him going. The desire for revenge.

He would avenge what Greg Rich and the Musketeers had done to him.

The door of the barn where he lay creaked open. Michel recoiled from the sunlight that spilled into the room.

"There's nothing to fear," his own voice told him. "It's only me."

Dominic Richelieu, his younger self, approached. Dominic had rescued Michel from the Gard River and found him this hayloft to hide in while he recovered. As he came to Michel's side, he tried to hide his disgust.

Michel understood why—his face was a hideous mask of scarred flesh—and yet Dominic's reaction made him seethe with anger. "Please tell me you've found something edible this time," he snarled.

"Carrots and beets." Dominic took them from the folds of his clothes.

"Fool!" Michel snapped. "You know I can't eat those things!" Somehow, even his stomach had been affected by the ordeal the Musketeers had put him through. He'd inhaled too much smoke—or maybe too much water—and hadn't been able to keep anything down for days.

"I thought you could try again," Dominic said.

"I need soup," Michel told him. "How hard is it to find

some soup? It's practically all anyone in this cursed time eats!"

"It's not that simple!" Dominic shot back angrily. "We are fugitives, thanks to you! You lost our army, our money, the Devil's Stone . . ."

"None of that was my fault!" Michel roared. "It was the Musketeers!"

"They are only boys, and yet you let the four of them defeat you and our entire army."

"And where were you during all that?"

"Doing exactly what you'd asked of me," Dominic said. "Keeping my distance and letting you handle things. You told me to trust you, that you could take care of everything. You said that under your leadership Paris and all of France would fall. Obviously, I was a fool to believe in you. Everything you have done has led only to failure."

Michel glared at his younger self. "All is not lost. I am healing. By tomorrow, I will be strong enough to travel again. We can make it to Paris."

"In your condition?" Dominic asked. "That will take weeks."

"If I were a mere mortal, perhaps. But I am not." Michel held up his hand as evidence. Although the skin had been badly blistered and burned just days before, it was beginning to return to its normal state. The healing had been much slower than Michel had hoped, but it *was* healing—whereas a normal human would have been scarred for life. "It will not be long before I look just like you again. And while I do not have all my strength back yet, with your help—and a few good horses—we can reach Paris in only a few days."

Dominic frowned in doubt. "And then what? We are wanted men there."

Michel waved his hand dismissively. "The king's guard does not concern me. Once we recover both halves of the Devil's Stone, we will be invincible. The stone, once united, can do the most incredible things."

"And what of the Musketeers?" Dominic asked. "Surely *they* must concern you. They have thwarted your plans twice now."

"They are of no consequence," Michel replied. "I have figured out how to defeat them once and for all."

"You keep saying that—and they keep defeating *us*," Dominic shot back.

Michel suddenly began to laugh. It was a ghastly sound, coming from his burned throat. "But this time will be different. It's a drastic measure, but it won't merely get rid of the Musketeers. . . . It will ensure they never existed at all."

PART ONE

THE FORTRESS

ONE

Les Baux de Provence
420 miles south of Paris
August 1615

In less than a day, Greg Rich would die.

So would his fellow Musketeers: Athos, Aramis, and Porthos. And Catherine as well. The four stood with him now in the pillory, mocked by passersby.

They were all being held prisoner in the town of Les Baux, a medieval village perched high on a rocky mesa. The village had only one entrance: a steep, narrow road that came up to a heavily fortified gate. Everywhere else, Les Baux was protected by cliffs of limestone that rose hundreds of feet from the swampy lowlands—a fetid, mosquito-ridden maze of marshy bogs. The surrounding mountains were some of the strangest Greg had ever seen, filled with gnarled rock formations.

Although Les Baux was in France, the local lord's allegiance was to the Prince of Condé, not to King Louis XIII. And so the Musketeers, as representatives of King Louis, were to be hung in a public spectacle. Then they would be decapitated. Their heads would be placed on pikes, while their bodies were thrown over the cliffs into the marshland below.

Greg and his friends had been in Les Baux for three days, brought there by Condé's men after Milady de Winter had engineered their capture. They had walked the thirty miles in a single day, forced to slog through the heat without food or rest and with barely any water. The journey had nearly killed Athos. His leg, wounded by an arrow in a surprise attack in Arles, was now swollen and badly infected.

Since arriving, they had spent their nights in cramped, frigid dungeon cells and their days in the pillory. In the town square, they were forced to stand for hours in the blazing sun, hunched over with a wooden frame locked around their wrists and neck, for all the people of Les Baux to see. Jeering townsfolk occasionally threw rotten vegetables at them.

It would have been miserable under any circumstances, but two things made it even worse for Greg.

First, he felt responsible for Catherine being here. He'd had a chance to save her, back at the Pont du Gard when he'd realized his fellow Musketeers were running into a trap. But in the heat of the moment, he hadn't thought to tell her to stay back or run away. Now she would die with them.

Second, he'd lost the trust of Athos and Porthos. He hadn't told them the truth about Michel Dinicoeur—that the man was immortal—until it was too late. Now they knew Greg must have lied to them about himself as well. Both obviously felt deceived, although Athos seemed far more upset. Between his wounded leg and his wounded pride—he'd been stunned when Milady, the woman he loved, had betrayed him—he was seething with anger, and he'd turned that on Greg.

"Athos, Porthos, this is ridiculous," Greg said as they stood in the pillory on the second day. "I've said I'm sorry a hundred times over. I should have been honest with you."

"Then why weren't you?" Porthos demanded.

"Because I was afraid this would be your reaction," Greg admitted. "And the longer I kept secrets from you, the harder it was to tell you. But now I'll tell you anything you want to know. We have to get past this."

"What does it matter?" Athos asked sullenly. "In a day, we'll all be dead."

"Not necessarily," Greg said. "When all of us have worked

as a team, we've done the impossible. We rescued my parents from a prison everyone said was impenetrable. The five of us turned back an entire army. If we put our minds together now, I'm sure we can figure out a way to escape."

Athos frowned in response, but Greg caught a flicker of something in his expression.

"You know it's true, don't you?" Greg asked. "I know that look of yours. You've been trying to work out an escape yourself."

"Of course I have," Athos admitted. "Who wouldn't? I don't want to die."

"Then don't," Aramis said. "You want to know the *real* reason he didn't tell you the truth about himself? I told him not to."

Athos and Porthos shifted their attention to Aramis. "Why?" both demanded.

"Because I didn't think you'd understand," Aramis said. "So if you're going to be angry at anyone, it should be me."

Athos frowned. Greg knew the swordsman was already angry at Aramis; both had vied for the affections of Milady de Winter, before she had betrayed them.

But Porthos gave in. "Who are you, really, D'Artagnan?"

"For one thing, my name isn't D'Artagnan. It's Greg. And I'm not from the Artagnan region of France. I'm from four hundred years in the future."

Porthos and Athos stared at Greg as though he might be insane. Then they looked to Aramis.

"It's true," the cleric told them.

"How is that possible?" Porthos asked.

"Michel Dinicoeur made it happen," Greg told him. "You see, Michel isn't Dominic Richelieu's twin brother. He *is* Dominic Richelieu. At some point in my past—which is actually *your* future—around 1630 or so, Dominic got hold of a magic amulet called the Devil's Stone. The stone is actually two pieces, and when you put them together, they have incredible power. Dominic used that power to make himself immortal and then tried to gain as much wealth as possible. He hoped to live forever as a rich and powerful man, but he was thwarted by the three of you."

Greg fell silent as some townspeople passed, not wanting them to hear his tale. "Down with King Louis!" the people hissed at them. "Death to all who support him!"

"The three of us?" Porthos asked once they were gone. "How?"

"I don't know all the details," Greg said. "But you know how Dinicoeur is missing his right hand? Athos did that to him."

"Well done!" Porthos said to Athos, and Greg thought he saw Athos crack a small smile.

"You all took the Devil's Stone from Dominic and locked him in the Bastille," Greg continued. "The Devil's Stone was broken back in two, and the pieces were separated so they could never be put together again. Meanwhile, Dominic sat in the Bastille for over a hundred years, plotting revenge against you three. Eventually, the Bastille was overthrown during a revolution and Dominic escaped. He changed his name to Michel Dinicoeur and eventually tracked down both pieces of the stone. I don't know where he found the first half, but the second was owned by my family . . . his descendants."

Catherine gasped, her eyes widening. Greg had shared much of his story with her before—but not this part. "You and Richelieu are related?"

Greg nodded. "From what I can tell, I'm his great-great-great-great-great-great-great-grandson. Or something like that. My family was supposed to protect their half of the amulet. Unfortunately, that message got lost over the centuries. Dinicoeur tricked my parents into thinking he was a museum curator at the Louvre in our time, and we brought the amulet to him—"

"Wait," Porthos said. "How could someone be a museum curator at the royal palace?"

"Well," Greg said, "in the future, the Louvre isn't the royal palace. It's a museum; one of the most famous museums in the world."

"If the Louvre is a museum, then where does the king of France live?" Porthos asked.

Greg grimaced, wishing he hadn't opened this can of worms. "There is no king of France anymore," he said.

"You mean France was overthrown?" Porthos gasped.

"No," Greg said. "France still exists. It's just ruled by the people."

"How could that possibly work?" Porthos asked.

"It does. You'll just have to trust me on this," Greg said. "The point is, Dinicoeur wanted to get even with all of you for what you'd done to him. His plan was to use the Devil's Stone to travel back in time and kill the three of you *before* you became the Three Musketeers. Then you wouldn't be around to defeat him—and his younger self, Richelieu, would be rich and powerful for eternity."

"But if Dinicoeur did that, wouldn't that negate his own existence?" Catherine asked. "If Richelieu is rich and powerful, then there's no reason for him to ever become Dinicoeur and travel back through time."

"I think that's perfectly fine with Dinicoeur," Greg said. "His life has been pretty miserable, thanks to all of you. In a sense, he's trying to reset history and start over. All he cares about is making sure Richelieu becomes immortal."

Porthos frowned. "Time travel can be awfully confusing to understand."

"Try *doing* it," Greg said. "It's not easy."

Porthos nodded empathically. "So how *did* you do it?"

"Once my family was at the Louvre, Dinicoeur snatched our half of the Devil's Stone," Greg said. "When he put both pieces together, the stone opened up a hole in time by making a portrait of the old Louvre come to life. Dinicoeur went through it and my family followed him."

"So that's how your family suddenly ended up in the palace that night?" Porthos asked. "The night Richelieu had your parents arrested and thrown in prison."

"Exactly," Greg said. "We didn't know we were jumping through time. We were just trying to get our family heirloom back. Unfortunately, the Devil's Stone got left in the future—and all of us need it. Dinicoeur needs it to make Richelieu immortal—and my family needs it to get back home through time again. That's what Dinicoeur has been doing: trying to recover both halves of the stone. He found the first somewhere in Spain—and, from what Aramis and I can tell, the second is back in Paris."

"If that's the case, then why didn't Dinicoeur get that one first?" Porthos asked.

"I have no idea," Greg admitted. "The best I can figure is that for some reason, Dinicoeur needs the first half to get the second."

"Do you have any idea where in Paris the second half is?" Porthos asked.

"Not exactly, but we've found some clues," Greg said. "Catherine once overheard Dinicoeur tell Richelieu that the stone was hidden under the king's nose."

"What's that supposed to mean?" Porthos asked.

"That the stone might be somewhere in the Louvre itself, I guess," Greg replied. "But then, on Dinicoeur's map, we found an inscription in Greek on the Île de la Cité about something called 'the Crown of Minerva.' Have you ever heard of that?"

Porthos shook his head, or at least tried to. It wasn't easy with the pillory cinched around his neck. "No. Does it have something to do with the stone?"

"I think so," Greg said.

"How could the stone be in the Louvre *and* on the Île de la Cité?" Catherine asked.

"I don't know," Greg admitted.

"Perhaps the stone has been broken into even more pieces," Catherine suggested. "One is in the palace and the other is near this Crown of Minerva."

"Maybe," Greg said with a grimace. The thought of tracking down *one* hidden piece of the stone was daunting enough, let alone two.

"What does it matter anyhow?" Athos asked angrily. It was the first thing he'd said since Greg had begun his story. "We don't have the first half of the stone—and neither does Dinicoeur. Milady de Winter does." He stared daggers at Greg. "You let her get it."

Only because you didn't listen to me and ran right into her trap, Greg thought, though he held his tongue. "I know. I'm sorry. The good news is, she doesn't really know anything about the stone. She only knows that it's powerful."

"But she'll figure out the rest," Athos said. "Milady's far

more clever than anyone realizes. Plus, she's probably half-way to Paris with Condé by now. Even if we could escape this place, we've lost too much time."

"We still have to try," Greg said. "If Condé sacks Paris and Milady gets all the pieces of the Devil's Stone . . ." What he wanted to say was, *All of human history will be changed*, but he knew that meant something to him and not to the others. He was the only one who knew what the future of the world held and how Milady or Dinicoeur could ruin it.

"It will be very bad news for France," Aramis finished. "And as Musketeers, it is our job to protect this country."

"I know what our job is," Athos shot back. "But we're not in any position to do it. La Mort wasn't the most impenetrable prison in France. Les Baux is. We're either locked out here in the pillory or in the dungeon. We're surrounded by an entire army of guards, and there's only one way out of the city."

Greg's eyes flicked toward the city gate. It was an imposing structure, built to keep enemies from getting into the city, but it would just as well prevent anyone from getting out. A dozen guards stood watch there, and an iron portcullis hung from it, ready to drop at the slightest hint of alarm.

"The only other way out of the city is over a cliff," Athos went on. "And since none of us knows how to fly, that option is out. So let's face the facts: We're not getting out of here."

"I don't believe that," Greg said. "If we all put our heads together and work as a team . . ."

"We're not a team," Athos said angrily. "Not anymore. Barring a miracle, tomorrow at dawn, we are going to die."

TWO

At dusk, the guards came to return the prisoners to their cells.

After eight hours of being hunched over in the pillory, Greg was thrilled to stand up straight and stretch his back, but the relief was short-lived. The guards clamped heavy chains around their ankles, wrists, and necks, then linked all the prisoners together front to back. They had to walk through a gauntlet of townspeople, who jeered, spat, and kicked them as they passed. "Behold the enemies of Condé!" the guards told the crowd. "This is what happens to those who will not support him!"

To the west, the sun dropped below the lip of the cliff, sinking into the swamp below. Greg wondered if it was the last sunset he'd ever see.

No, he told himself. Even if Athos and the others were resigned to their fate, he couldn't be. There was too much at stake. The Prince of Condé couldn't be allowed to overthrow King Louis. Neither Milady nor Dinicoeur could be allowed to obtain the entire Devil's Stone. If any of those things happened, the history of the world—the events that had led to the future Greg was from—would be irrevocably altered. Greg had no idea how to prevent any of that from happening, but he had to try. And the first step was figuring out how to escape. There was no chance that anyone was coming to help them; no one even knew where they were. If the Musketeers were going to get out of Les Baux, they'd have to do it themselves.

Keep your eyes open, Greg thought. *Don't let anything escape your attention. Somehow, somewhere, there is a way out of here.*

He lifted his head as high as he could with the chains hanging from his neck and tried to ignore the taunts and blows of the townsfolk and concentrate on his surroundings.

They were heading uphill toward the castle, which loomed above the center of town and, among other things, housed the dungeon where they would spend the night. Although he loathed the place, Greg had to admit the castle was rather amazing. Some of the lower floors inside were belowground—carved directly into the mountain itself. Entire rooms and stairwells hadn't been built so much as sculpted. The upper floors had been made with the excavated stone, so that the castle appeared to be an extension of the rock it sat on. It perched at the very edge of the mesa, its southern wall flush with the cliff below.

The castle was much newer and far better constructed than the Louvre palace, with tall turrets and ramparts and large windows. Every facet was bright and clean. It was almost a relief to pass from the dirty, noisy outside tumult into the clean, quiet entry chamber. And the entry paled in comparison to what came next: the banquet hall.

As they made their way into the hall, Greg noticed that it was designed to impress guests, to signal that the lord of Les Baux was a man of great standing. It was built on the southern side of the castle, so that its large windows offered impressive views of the lord's lands. Anyone standing before them had a commanding view of the surrounding countryside for thirty miles—although there was a vertiginous drop to the swamp at the bottom of the cliff. The room was huge, with a banquet table large enough to seat fifty people, flanked at either end by huge fireplaces big enough to roast entire cattle in. A vaulted ceiling soared four stories above, and a grand stone staircase swept around the northern edge of the room to a wide interior mezzanine on the east.

Most impressive of all, however, was the chandelier. It was the largest Greg had ever seen, a huge wheel of wood suspended by a long, thick rope that threaded through an iron ring in the center of the ceiling and then wound around a winch on the main floor. Nearly a thousand candles sat on the wheel, and when lit, they were spectacular. In 1615, once the sun went down, most rooms—even those in the Louvre—were generally dim and full of shadows. But with all the candles lit, the banquet hall was as bright as day.

The chandelier, thought Greg. As he stared up at it, an idea began to form in his mind. . . .

"Ah, hello, my dear prisoners!"

Greg shifted his gaze to the mezzanine, where Lord Contingnac, ruler of Les Baux, now looked down on them. He was a rotund man with a big black beard and a wide belly, who always seemed to take great joy in making others suffer.

"It looks like your hangings are going to be quite the event tomorrow!" Contingnac crowed smugly. "The whole town is very excited to see them!"

Athos glared at the lord. "It should be your neck that hangs tomorrow for treason, not ours," he said.

Contingnac laughed. "Oh, that's good. Say something like that tomorrow on the gallows. The people will then love it even more when you die!" He paraded down the grand staircase, his eyes fixed on the prisoners. "It is *your* king and all his followers who have committed treason," he

15

said. "Louis is not the rightful ruler of France. Rather than take the throne, he should have abdicated to Condé."

"Will our deaths tomorrow be an example of the way Condé will rule France?" Aramis asked pointedly. "Does he plan to torture and kill all who don't agree with him? Anyone who has to frighten the populace into following him isn't a leader. He's a despot. I would rather die for a good king than kneel to a tyrant."

Contingnac's smile faded. "Condé has no need to frighten anyone," he snarled. "My people love him."

"They fear him," Porthos said. "Condé is nothing but a power-hungry madman. Long live Louis! Long live the king!"

Aramis and Athos took up the cry. Before Greg knew it, he and Catherine were shouting as well. After three days of being treated so poorly, the moment of defiance was an incredible release. Their voices echoed through the banquet hall and out into the town. And for a few brief moments, Greg felt alive and free again.

Then the guards were on them. A fist slammed into Greg's stomach, quieting him and doubling him over. To his side, Aramis was thrown to the floor. Another guard backhanded Catherine so hard that she fell. Athos and Porthos continued to make a stand, however, fending off the guards despite their chains. Throughout, they continued chanting. "Long live the king! Long live the king!"

"Silence, you fools!" roared Contingnac. "Your precious king will not live much longer than any of you. Soon,

Condé's army will breach the walls of Paris, the prince and his betrothed will take the throne, and the glory of France will finally be restored!"

To Greg's surprise, these words did to Athos what all the guards couldn't: They took the fight out of him. His defiance suddenly faded, replaced by shock and sorrow, and Contingnac's men quickly took him down.

Several pairs of hands grabbed Greg roughly and dragged him to his feet. The guards shoved him and the other prisoners out of the banquet hall, through the kitchen, and down another, less grand set of stairs. These wound downward into the rooms that had been chiseled directly into the mountain. Here were the granaries, armories, and storage rooms. Unlike the bright white rooms above, these rooms were dark and tomblike, filled with dripping water, bats, and rats. They were places deemed unfit for any humans to spend much time in.

Except prisoners.

The dungeon was down here as well. The cells weren't really rooms so much as cramped spaces that had been dug into the rock. There were three of them, each less than four feet high. The guards unlocked the chains from their prisoners, then forced Porthos and Athos into the first cell, Catherine into the second, and Aramis and Greg into the third. Inside, the floor and walls were so rough-hewn, the space was little better than a cave. There was barely enough room for both boys—and no comfortable place to sit or lie down. There was only a thin slit in the cliff side to allow in fresh air and sunlight, and now that the sun had set, there was no light but the guards' torches. When the thick wooden door slammed, that disappeared as well— and Greg and Aramis were plunged into darkness.

The stone walls and door were so thick, it was almost impossible to hear anything outside—although Greg thought he could detect the faint sound of Catherine crying.

He felt like crying himself. It wasn't merely that death waited for him the next morning. It was the fact that even if he did miraculously escape, the chances of him ever setting things right and getting back to his own time seemed almost impossible.

To start with, he didn't merely need both halves of the Devil's Stone to get home. He also needed his phone—and Milady had that. When Greg had traveled to the past, the Devil's Stone had turned a painting of the Louvre in 1615 into a portal to that time. So to get back, he needed a photo from the twenty-first century—and the only photos he had were on his phone. But Milady had taken it, thinking it was some powerful magical object from the future.

Everything of importance to Greg had been taken from him. He'd been stripped of the rest of his belongings upon being taken prisoner. The only thing he'd managed to hold on to were his matches.

He had only two left, wrapped in a small piece of oilskin to keep them dry. He'd palmed them when Condé's men had frisked him for weapons. Since matches wouldn't be invented for another two hundred fifty years, they were quite valuable—and indeed, they'd come in handy before. Greg wouldn't have been able to rescue his parents from prison without them. He had secreted the remaining two in a fold of his clothes again, expecting that they might be useful at some point—although they certainly weren't of any use now. This small cell was freezing, but there was nothing in it to burn for warmth.

Greg tried to focus on escape. He thought about everything he had just experienced, everything he had just seen and heard. Somewhere in there, he thought, there was useful information. Clues to aid in their escape. He simply had to put them all together.

But he came up blank. His mind kept turning to all the problems that awaited him outside Les Baux. He had so many enemies to confront. Richelieu and Dinicoeur, seeking the Devil's Stone and the power that came with it. Milady and Condé, plotting to oust the king. And Condé had an entire army at his disposal. Greg had overheard Contingnac boast of it. Condé had been building the army for months near the German border. It was now advancing on Paris from the east, threatening to overthrow King Louis and alter the course of history forever.

It seemed so daunting. How could Greg and his friends possibly triumph over all that? Even Athos, who was never cowed by anything, had given up hope.

Greg realized that despite all the odds against him, the most disheartening thing was how upset his friends were with him. The Musketeers had become the best friends he'd ever had. And now . . .

"Athos still seems angry at me," Greg said.

"Yes," Aramis agreed.

"But I told him the truth, just like he wanted me to."

"I know, but I don't think this is about the truth. It's about trust. Loyalty is extremely important to Athos. I fear I made a terrible mistake when I advised you not to tell him the truth about yourself. Now that he feels you betrayed him, it may take a very long time to earn his trust back."

"But I didn't betray him nearly as badly as Milady did," Greg argued.

"That's true," Aramis admitted. "And my guess is, what Milady did to him stings far worse than what you did. But since you're here, you're bearing the brunt of his resentment."

Greg nodded sadly. "What do you think it was that Contingnac said that upset Athos so much?" he asked. "It wasn't news that Condé intends to take Paris."

"No, but it *was* news that Condé has a fiancée." In the darkness, Aramis sounded like he'd lost all hope as well, and suddenly, Greg understood why.

"Milady?" he asked. "She's engaged to Condé?"

"Who else could it be?" Aramis sighed heavily. "And she

actually made me think she cared for me. I was such a fool."

"No, you weren't," Greg began.

"I *was*," Aramis countered. "Athos and I both were. Milady tricked us, played us off each other, made us blind to what she was really up to. She worked us like puppets. Got us to engineer the fall of Paris. . . ."

"Paris hasn't fallen," Greg said. "Not yet."

"But it will soon," Aramis said. "If the king paid any attention to the message I sent—at Milady's urging—then the French army has left the city, leaving it vulnerable to attack."

"It made sense to send that message," Greg said. "The Spanish army was attacking from the south, and Dominic knew of secret entrances into Paris. The fact that we repelled it was a miracle."

"Even so, she used us. And all along, she hasn't just been working to give Condé the throne. She's going to have a throne herself—as queen." Aramis spat. "I'll bet she doesn't love Condé, either. He's just another dupe she's tricked into servicing her rise to power. And now she's after the Devil's Stone as well. If she gets that *and* France, she'll be the most powerful leader the world has seen since Julius Caesar."

"Well, she doesn't have either yet," Greg told him. "First of all, Paris may still hold. Some of the army must have remained in the city. And there's still the wall."

"But Milady knows how to get past the wall," Aramis said.

Now Greg groaned. Richelieu's map. It showed the locations of three different secret entrances into Paris—and Milady had it. "At least she doesn't know where the other half of the stone is," he said.

"No, but as Athos suggested, if anyone can find it, she can. And even if she doesn't, Dinicoeur is still out there, and he *knows* where the other half is for sure."

Greg straightened up in the darkness. "You really think he's still alive?"

"He's immortal. He *can't* die."

"I know, but . . . I guess I thought there was still a way he could be killed." Greg thought back to what had happened to Michel Dinicoeur at the Pont du Gard. "The man was hit by several arrows, set on fire, then fell off a bridge into a raging river. If he survived that, he must be in terrible shape."

"That's the downside to immortality that no one ever thinks of," Aramis said. "Man was not meant to live forever. Not in this form, at least."

Greg thought about that. Was it really possible that Dinicoeur would exist forever? That he'd be around in billions of years, long after the sun had burned out and humanity was gone? "I suppose that's another reason he'd want the stone, then. If he could make himself immortal with it, he could make himself mortal again as well."

"Yes," Aramis agreed. "But for now, he is far more concerned with the short term. And so I think we can assume that he is heading for Paris as well."

Greg sighed. Now he had *two* clever adversaries with a head start in the race to the Devil's Stone—and an enemy army closing in on Paris. "All the more reason for us to get out of here."

Aramis laughed. A hollow, mocking laugh that echoed ominously in the dungeon. "Don't waste your last hours on earth chasing pipe dreams."

"It's not a pipe dream," Greg argued. "There must be a way."

"Really? How do you plan to escape this cell? The walls are solid rock. We can't dig through them. And that door is impenetrable as well."

"Then we'll have to wait until the guards open the door in the morning. There'll be some time before they can chain us up again."

"A few seconds at best," Aramis said sullenly. "During which time we are outnumbered and unarmed. Athos tried to fight back our first morning here, remember? All he ended up doing was earning us extra time in the pillory."

"So then we don't fight," Greg said. "We get them to drop their guard and catch them by surprise instead."

"How?"

"I don't know. Maybe when they come in the morning, you and I could pretend like we're dead." Greg frowned as he said it, knowing that wasn't very original. It was just the first thing that popped into his head.

But Aramis sat up, intrigued. "That's not a bad idea," he said.

"Really?" Greg asked. *Because it happens all the time in the movies,* he thought. But then he caught himself. There weren't any movies yet. There were barely any books. Anything he thought was a cliché, something that had been done a thousand times in the future, hadn't been done yet in 1615.

"Yes," Aramis said. "How would it work?"

"Well, we'd just lie here when the guards came for us in the morning," Greg explained. "They'd see us and think we were dead, so they'd drag us out of here without putting the chains on us first . . . and that's when we'd be able to get the jump on them. Hopefully, we'd be able to free the others, too."

"But then what?" The sullenness had returned to Aramis's voice. "We'd still have to get out of the castle, through the entire town, and past the gate. There'll be a hundred guards along the way, if not more. We won't be able to catch every one of them by surprise."

Greg nodded gravely, but then his thoughts returned to the massive chandelier in the banquet hall, and he realized what had intrigued him about it. A smile quickly spread across his face. "I think we *can* surprise them all," he said. "I know how to get out of Les Baux."

THREE

THE HOURS DRAGGED UNTIL MORNING. AFTER GREG HAD shared his plan with Aramis, there was nothing they could do but wait. He tried to sleep, but the stony floor was too cold and uncomfortable, and besides, his mind was racing. Even with a good plan, escape would be difficult; there were a thousand things that could go wrong. To make things worse, there was no way to discuss it with the others. Greg could only hope that once he and Aramis put things in motion, the others would be quick to respond.

As he lay there, he found himself thinking about his

parents. It had been weeks since he'd seen them. Now, if Greg ended up dead in Les Baux, his parents would never know what had happened to him; he'd simply vanish without a trace. Similarly, he had no idea what was happening with his parents. Were they all right in Paris? Had Greg's father found any clues to the location of the Devil's Stone? If Greg didn't survive, did they have any hope of making it home without him?

After several hours, thinking of every eventuality in his escape plan—every possible thing that could go wrong—and how to deal with it, he finally gave in to exhaustion and fell asleep.

It seemed like only a minute later when he heard the rattle of keys in his cell door.

His eyes snapped open. Through the tiny slit of a window, he could see the faintest trace of light in the eastern sky.

"Aramis!" he whispered in the dark. "Are you ready?"

"Yes," came the reply. "God be with us."

The door swung open and torchlight spilled into the room. Greg held perfectly still, keeping his eyes open with the empty stare of a dead man. On the floor close by, Aramis did the same.

In the hall outside, he could hear the other cell doors opening, the rattle of chains, the distant voices of his friends.

"Get up, you two," a guard snarled. He was a huge, cruel

man named Jean who had never hesitated to treat the boys roughly.

Greg and Aramis didn't move.

"Did you hear me?" Jean roared. "I said get up!" The guard had to practically double himself over to get into the cell. He smacked Greg's leg with a thick hand.

Greg felt the pain, but didn't so much as flinch.

"What the . . . ?" Jean now sounded confused. He waved his torch in front of the boys and stared at their glassy eyes.

Greg could feel Jean's horrid breath on his face, but still he didn't move.

"What's going on in there?" another guard shouted from the hall.

"I think they're dead," Jean replied.

"What?" the other guard asked, and Greg thought he could hear Athos, Porthos, and Catherine cry out in alarm as well. "How can that be?"

"I don't know. They're just dead," Jean replied.

"Well, get them out of there," the second guard said. "We can still put their heads on pikes."

Jean backed out of the cell, grabbed Greg's ankles with one meaty hand, and dragged him out the door. Greg's head bounced along the rough stone floor, but he kept himself rigid. He gazed blankly upward as Jean and the second guard—Simon—loomed over him, waving a torch in his face.

Out of the corner of his eye, Greg could see more guards

roughly handling his friends, who were looking toward him with horror. Catherine was wailing. A guard forced her up against the wall to clap her chains on.

Greg felt horrible for what he was doing to her—and to the others. He wanted to signal them that he was fine, that everything would be all right. But he couldn't. The time wasn't right yet.

"Get the other one," Simon told Jean. Jean stepped over Greg to enter the cell again.

Jean slid Aramis out of the cell and tumbled him into Greg's side.

Down the hall, the guards had put the chains on Athos, too, but Porthos hadn't been shackled yet. The guards were too distracted, looking at Greg and Aramis with morbid fascination.

Simon and Jean bent over Aramis to examine him for signs of life. Jean waved the torch in Aramis's face. Greg noticed Simon's sword and keys dangling from his belt.

Now or never, Greg thought.

In a flash, he was on his feet. He wrenched Simon's sword from its hilt, slashing through the brute's belt at the same time. The guard's pants dropped to his ankles, and his keys clattered to the floor.

Simon and Jean swung toward Greg, and he saw actual terror in their eyes. Their first reaction hadn't been that he'd been faking his death, but that he'd actually been dead and had somehow come back to life. Greg threw himself at

weapons clattered to the floor.

Athos and Porthos knocked both men unconscious.

Athos grabbed one sword, then tossed the other to Catherine.

Now that Greg was safe, Aramis slashed the rope free from the chandelier. "Help me!" he yelled.

The others rushed to his aid. The rope was so long, they each had to coil a few lengths over their shoulders to carry it all, but thankfully, it wasn't terribly heavy and they hurried up the stairs with it. On the mezzanine, Athos paused by Greg's side to confront Contingnac, who was now sniveling with fear. "I see you're not so tough when *your* neck is on the line," Athos said.

"Please don't kill me," Contingnac whimpered. "I'll do anything you want."

"Good. We could use a hostage." Athos grabbed the lord by the hair, pulled him to his feet, and placed his blade to the man's throat. "How do we get to the top of the south wall?"

Contingnac led the way, Athos keeping the blade on him. The others followed with the rope. They quickly made their way through the castle and up a series of staircases until they reached the roof. A parapet ran around the entire circumference, marked every few feet by merlons, which were raised portions of the wall that soldiers could take cover behind when firing on the enemy. The staircase emerged on the northern wall of the castle, which looked down onto the town. Below them, the Musketeers could see Contingnac's army amassing, alerted by the calls that the prisoners had escaped. However, just as Greg had figured, the soldiers assumed the prisoners would go toward the city gate, so they had headed there as well, forming a daunting barricade that the Musketeers would never have breached.

The soldiers at the gate kept their eyes riveted to the doors of the castle. No one even thought to look up toward the roof. After all, going there would be heading into a dead end. Thus, in the murky light of dawn, the boys' presence atop the castle went unnoticed by anyone below.

There were three guards stationed on the parapet—but the moment they saw Contingnac held prisoner, they dropped their weapons. The Musketeers bound and gagged each quickly with strips of cloth torn from the soldiers' own uniforms.

They finally reached the southern side of the castle. Greg peered over the edge. There was nothing but a sheer drop below: four stories of castle, followed by a great deal of cliff. Greg couldn't be sure exactly how high it was, as the base of the cliff was obscured by morning mist that hovered over the swamp below.

"You want us to climb down *that*?" Porthos asked worriedly.

"It's either climb down this rope now or hang from one later," Greg replied.

"Good point," Porthos said. "Let's get going."

The Musketeers quickly unwound the coiled rope from their bodies, piling it onto the walkway. Greg looped one end around a merlon and began tying knots in it. He remembered how to tie a decent bowline from the Boy Scouts and knew that in theory, only one should have been sufficient, but seeing as his life was soon going to depend on that rope, he decided to tie a few more, just to be safe.

Then Contingnac struck. Athos's infected leg had gotten even worse during the night, and the morning's exertion had taken its toll on the swordsman. Overwhelmed by the pain, he'd dropped his guard for a second while uncoiling the rope—and that was all the time Contingnac needed. The lord drove a knee into Athos's wound, and when the Musketeer cried out in pain, Contingnac snatched the sword from his grip and turned it on Catherine.

"Stand down!" he warned the Musketeers as they reached for their weapons. "One move from you and I slit her throat!"

The Musketeers had no choice but to raise their arms in surrender.

"They're up here!" Contingnac bellowed to his soldiers. "On the southern wall!"

By now, most of the soldiers had amassed at the city gate on the far side of town, but Les Baux was only a few blocks across, and Contingnac's voice carried well through the still morning air, echoing off the surrounding hills with such volume that he might as well have fired a cannon.

Greg watched the army react. It took a few moments for the soldiers to leap into action, swarming toward the castle like ants. Greg knew it wouldn't take more than a few minutes for them to cross the town and scale the castle, and once they did, the Musketeers would be trapped.

"Hurry!" Contingnac roared to his men. "They're going to—"

Before he could finish, Catherine drove an elbow into his kidney, catching him by surprise. As Contingnac groaned in pain, she slipped free from his grasp. Enraged, Contingnac lunged at her with his sword, but Catherine sidestepped the attack, and the lord's momentum carried him into the low railing along the walkway. All it took was a nudge from Athos, and Contingnac toppled over the edge. He screamed in horror as he tumbled all the way down, bouncing off the limestone wall a few times before disappearing into the mist.

"Nicely done," Porthos told Catherine.

Catherine herself was stunned by what had happened. "I was just trying to escape," she said. "I didn't mean for him to . . ."

"Better him than us," Athos said. "Come on. We have work to do!"

"Drop the rope!" Greg said, finishing his fourth knot.

"Are you sure that will hold us?" Aramis asked warily.

"I am," Greg said, though deep down, he was worried himself.

The Musketeers pitched the rope over the edge of the parapet. Greg watched it uncoil as it tumbled through the air and then slap into the cliff face with a loud *crack*. The far end disappeared into the swamp mist.

"Think it reaches all the way to the ground?" Athos asked.

"We're about to find out," Porthos replied.

An arrow suddenly bounced off the rampart beside him. A team of soldiers had found a point on the mesa that afforded them a direct line at the Musketeers. They were quite far away and arrows weren't tremendously accurate, but Greg still felt panic begin to creep in. There was no time to unknot the rope and move it to a safer position. They would just have to hope for the best.

"Let's go!" Greg cried, then looked at Catherine. "Ladies first."

Catherine turned to him, worry in her eyes. "I'm not sure I can. . . ."

"Right now, it's safer on that rope than it is up here," Greg told her. As he spoke, another arrow whistled past, as if to prove his point. "You'll be okay. I promise."

He took Catherine's hand and gave it what he hoped was a reassuring squeeze.

Catherine nodded, scrambled over the parapet, and began climbing down. Aramis went next, and then Porthos and Athos insisted Greg go. There was no time to argue. As more arrows sailed through the air, Greg grabbed the rope and lowered himself over the wall.

The moment he was on the other side, his plan began to seem like the worst idea he'd ever had. He'd done some rock climbing back in modern times, but he'd never been this high up and not without any sort of safety gear. The ground somehow looked even farther away than it had before, a terrifying distance below. The rope seemed too thin to hold him, let alone five people, and a harsh, cold wind slammed into him and numbed his fingers, making holding on almost impossible. But there was no turning back. Contingnac's men were on their way—and once they arrived on the parapet, anyone still dangling from the rope would be a sitting duck. *The faster you get down,* Greg told himself, *the faster this nightmare will be over.*

He cinched his legs around the rope and lowered himself as quickly as possible, trying not to look down. The wind twirled him and slammed him into the rock face over and over, but he sucked up the pain and pressed on. As difficult as the descent was for him, he knew it was even harder for Athos, who was now on the rope above him; who could barely use his wounded leg and thus had to bear most of his weight with his arms.

The rope jounced as Porthos clambered onto it. With the added weight of the portly Musketeer, Greg thought he could feel the whole thing starting to tear apart, but perhaps that was only his imagination.

He kept going, passing the base of the castle and reaching the solid rock of the cliff. And yet it didn't feel like he'd made any progress at all. The ground still seemed like it was miles away. He was still high enough that if he fell, he'd die.

From above, the roar of the soldiers grew louder. Greg gulped. Climbing down was taking far longer than he'd hoped. Contingnac's men had to be close to the parapet by now. He glanced up, but all he could see were Athos and Porthos above him. Too far above him. Athos was going much too slowly.

"Athos!" Greg yelled. "You need to move faster!"

"I'm going as fast as I can!" Athos yelled back. "This isn't easy with only one good leg!"

"I don't suppose you could let me past you, then?" Porthos asked, only half joking.

Greg pushed himself to go faster, sliding down the rope even though it tore through his pants, burned his legs, and rubbed his palms raw. The rock of the cliff slid past him. Finally, he felt like he was getting close to the bottom, although the ground was still obscured by the mist.

He glanced up again. High above Athos and Porthos, at the top of the wall, several soldiers suddenly peered over the edge. Though Greg was far below them, there was now enough daylight that he could see their astonished faces. A second later, the rope jangled.

They're cutting it, Greg thought.

"We're down!" Aramis's voice rang up from the mist below. "It's not much farther!"

"Get clear!" Greg warned. "We might end up landing on you!"

The rope jounced again. Above Greg, Athos realized he had to move faster. He wrapped his wounded leg around the rope and slid, roaring with pain.

An arrow whizzed past Greg's head. It wasn't enough that the soldiers were trying to cut them loose; they were trying to shoot them as well.

He dropped into the mist and suddenly saw the ground. It was blessedly close—although, to his dismay, the rope didn't reach all the way to it. It ended a good ten feet above the swamp. Greg simply had to let go and hope for the best. He landed on uneven, spongy ground covered by six inches of frigid water. His feet slipped out from under him, and he tumbled into the muck. He staggered back to his feet, now soaked, cold, and muddy, but he didn't care; he'd never been so happy to feel the earth beneath him.

"D'Artagnan! Over here!" Catherine called. Greg spotted her and Aramis, taking shelter from the arrows under a small lip of rock in the cliff face. Greg raced to their side. To his surprise, Catherine threw her arms around him. "It worked," she whispered in his ear. "You did it."

"Not quite yet." Greg glanced up into the mist above, wondering where Athos and Porthos were. He could hear

Athos crying out in pain as he descended, but he still sounded too high. It couldn't take the soldiers that much longer to cut through the rope. . . .

Athos suddenly appeared in the mist about twenty feet up, coming down fast with Porthos above him. Greg heaved a sigh of relief.

There was a roar of triumph from high above—and the rope suddenly went slack.

Athos and Porthos plummeted the final distance, landing in the swamp with a splash. Both tumbled onto their backs and lay where they'd landed, unmoving.

Greg, Aramis, and Catherine rushed to their side. Greg reached Porthos first and found the Musketeer's eyes clamped shut. "Are you all right?" he asked.

"I've been better." Porthos's eyes snapped open, and he flashed a smile.

Greg realized, to his relief, that the soft, spongy ground had probably saved his friends, cushioning their landing. "Athos?" he asked.

Athos sat up and grimaced in pain. "I can move," he said through gritted teeth.

"Then let's go." Aramis helped Athos to his feet and lent his body as support. The two of them hurried into the misty swamp. Greg, Catherine, and Porthos followed right behind them. They were soon out of range of the soldiers' arrows, the mist covering their escape.

"Any chance they'll climb down after us?" Aramis asked.

"I doubt it," Porthos said. "First, they've just cut the only rope in town that's long enough. And second, the only reason anyone would make that climb was if their life depended on it."

"They'll still be coming for us, though," Athos warned.

"Yes," Greg said. "But they'll have to go out the gate on the far side of the mountain and come all the way around. And they'll have to do it on foot. Horses can't move through this swamp—and it's nearly impossible to track anyone through it. We'll have a huge head start on them, and they won't know which way we've gone."

Athos nodded. To Greg, it looked as though he might actually be impressed, but was trying not to show it.

"Which way *should* we go?" Catherine asked.

"East," Greg suggested. "The mountains rise that way, which means the swamp ends. There are more towns in the hills. We'll get to one, find some horses, and ride for Paris."

"Sounds like a plan," Porthos said, and the others nodded agreement.

They slogged on through the swamp. As Greg's wet clothes clung to him, he suddenly thought of his matches. He pulled out the oilskin to find that water had seeped into it. One of the matches was ruined. Meaning he only had one left.

The rising sun suddenly sliced through the mist, warming

them as they ran. Catherine turned to Greg. "If it weren't for you, we'd be hanging right now," she said. "You've saved us all."

Greg returned her smile, but the truth was, he felt only the tiniest bit of relief. Yes, they were alive, but they still had Dinicoeur, Richelieu, Milady de Winter, and all of Condé's army to confront. And before they could even do that, they had a long way to go—and they were already exhausted, famished, weak, and wounded.

The Musketeers plunged onward into the valley, heading toward Paris. To succeed in their mission seemed almost impossible, and Greg wondered if he would ever get home.

PART TWO

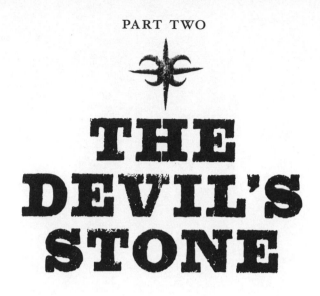

THE
DEVIL'S
STONE

✠— FOUR

Saint Sauveur, France
Eighty miles south of Paris

THE MUSKETEERS ENCOUNTERED THE FRENCH ARMY AT
the end of their third day of riding. Greg had no idea how
far they'd come; they'd stolen five horses from a small town
near Les Baux and had been riding almost nonstop ever
since. They had returned to the Pont du Gard, picked up
the ancient Roman road, and stayed on it the entire way
north. When the first horses had grown tired and balked
at going any farther, the Musketeers had simply traded
them for others. They had slept in barns and eaten only
what they could scrounge.

Greg had hoped to find the army on the Roman road. Seeing as it was the only major land route from Paris to the south—and there weren't enough boats in France to send the whole army down the Rhône—it made sense the army would be coming this way. If anything, Greg was annoyed the army hadn't gotten farther. It had been well over a week since the Musketeers had sent the urgent messages to Paris saying that the Spanish had invaded. Given that the soldiers had no way of knowing the Spanish had actually been repelled since then, Greg had expected them to be pushing south as fast as possible. Instead, however, the army was obviously taking its time. They hadn't covered even a quarter of the distance to the Pont du Gard yet.

Greg had thought that his trip south through France, when they'd been on a boat on the Rhône, had been difficult, but that was a vacation compared to this. His muscles ached from riding, and he'd been jouncing up and down for so long, he felt as though he'd scrambled his brains. After the first day, he was miserable—and it only got worse from there. But no one complained. Their enemies had a big head start on them, so the Musketeers had a great deal of time to make up.

Besides, Greg knew that as bad as he felt, Athos was even worse off. Athos's thigh was now so inflamed that it wouldn't fit in his pants leg. He'd had to turn his pants into shorts. Now Greg could see his friend's leg, baking in the sun as they rode. The area around the wound was beet red, while the wound itself was oozing pus. The pain was obviously intense and taking its toll, but Athos merely gritted his teeth through it.

"Maybe you should stop," Greg had counseled Athos during their second night on the road. "Your leg is in bad shape, and you're only making it worse."

Athos had scowled at him in response. While Porthos's distrust of Greg had softened after he'd engineered their escape from Les Baux, Athos still remained prickly around him. "I can handle it," he said.

"Your leg is badly infected, Athos. If you don't take care of it, you'll die."

"Are you a physician in the future, D'Artagnan?"

"No," Greg admitted. "But I know what I'm telling you is true."

"When we make it to Paris, I'll see a *real* physician," Athos shot back, and then rolled over to sleep, ending any further conversation.

After a few hours of riding the next day, his leg had obviously been hurting even worse, but Athos stubbornly refused to show the slightest sign of weakness. He rode just as hard as the rest of them, although Greg could see that he was sweating profusely and his gaze was getting glassy. If they hadn't found the French army, Greg suspected that Athos might have ridden until he died in the saddle.

The army was spread out in a field along the side of a

small creek. Compared to the Spanish army that Michel Dinicoeur had commanded, it was small and undisciplined. There were less than a thousand men, and even though there were still a few hours left in the day to march, they had already struck camp. Their tents were arranged haphazardly. Rather than spend the precious daylight training, the men lazed on the grass or played cards. No sentries were posted. Greg got the sense that if this army had encountered Dinicoeur's, it would have been massacred.

Most of the soldiers didn't even look up as the Musketeers approached. Greg figured that he and his friends didn't seem like much of a threat. After their hard journey, their clothes had been reduced to little more than rags. The boys were caked with dust from the road and damp with sweat from the heat. At best, they probably looked like local peasants who were seeking handouts. Only one soldier, whose uniform indicated he was an officer of some sort, even went on guard. "Who approaches the French army?" he asked, his sword drawn.

"The Musketeers," Aramis replied.

At the mention of "Musketeers," many other soldiers looked toward them.

"*You* are the Musketeers?" the officer asked doubtfully, but his expression changed to recognition once Athos turned toward him. "Athos!" he cried, at once happy to see his friend and disturbed by his appearance.

Athos used the last of his strength to muster a smile. "Hello, Emil," he said—and then toppled off his horse.

The other Musketeers dismounted and raced to his side, as did Emil. Greg rolled Athos over and felt his forehead. It was so hot, Greg guessed he had a high fever. "He needs water!"

Emil uncapped his own canteen and handed it to Greg. "What happened to him?" the officer demanded.

"He was wounded some days ago," Aramis reported. "But he has refused any medical help."

Emil turned to the closest soldier. "Fetch the camp physician, now!" While the soldier scurried away, Emil turned back to Aramis. "Athos and I are old friends. We started in the king's guard together. Tell me everything that happened to you."

Greg tipped the canteen to Athos's lips. His friend's eyes had fogged over, as though he was now delirious from the fever. Greg checked his pulse. Luckily, Athos's heart was still beating strongly. If anything, it was racing. Perhaps his fever was driving it faster.

While Greg gave Athos water, Aramis quickly filled Emil in on the Musketeers' adventures, from how they'd managed to turn back the Spanish army to their betrayal by Milady de Winter to their escape from Les Baux. By the time he'd finished, it seemed that half the camp had gathered to hear the tale.

"That is quite an adventure," Emil said when it was all

over. "You know for a fact that the Spanish army has completely disbanded?"

"We talked to a few people in the countryside after we escaped Les Baux," Aramis replied. "The Spaniards turned and fled back home, while anyone else who had joined their cause abandoned it."

"Unbelievable," Emil said, impressed. "An entire army repelled by four boys."

"And one girl." Greg nodded toward Catherine, who blushed modestly.

Emil shook his head. "How brave you were to face five hundred men."

"Five hundred?" Porthos asked, surprised. "It was over two thousand."

Emil looked at him curiously. "Your message to the king said five hundred."

"We sent no such message," Aramis said.

"Certainly you did," Emil told him. "It stated the size and position of the army, then laid out plans for counterattack in great detail. You even suggested what size army we would need. We certainly wouldn't have sent a force this small up against two thousand men!"

Greg and Aramis exchanged a look of understanding. "It was Milady," Aramis said.

"How's that?" Porthos asked.

"Remember when our homing pigeons were all released in Arles?" Greg said. "We all assumed that Valois had released them so we wouldn't be able to communicate with Paris. But Milady must have simply taken them instead."

"Then she sent false information to the king," Aramis continued. "Only, it would have looked like it came from *us*."

"But it would have been in *her* handwriting," Porthos said.

"True, but she could have faked mine, or perhaps even just used hers and said she was writing at my behest," Aramis explained. "As far as Paris knew, she was on our side."

"But why would she do such a thing?" Emil asked.

"Two reasons," Greg said. "First, she wanted to get the French army out of Paris. And second, she had no idea that we'd repel the Spanish. She probably hoped that the two armies would clash. The French army would be crushed while the Spanish army would be weakened."

"But to what end?" Emil inquired.

"So there would be no one to defend Paris against Condé's army," Greg answered.

"Condé?" Emil gasped in shock. "He has an army?"

"He claims he does," Aramis replied.

"How big is it?" Emil demanded. "And *where* is it?"

"We don't know," Aramis said sadly. "But our guess is that it is close to Paris now. How many soldiers are left in the city?"

"Only a residual force," Emil admitted, shaking his head with concern. "Perhaps a hundred. Maybe two. Although the city has very strong fortifications. . . ."

"Which Milady may know how to get around," Aramis said.

Emil reacted with surprise to this, but before he could ask any more, Porthos asked, "How far are we from Paris?"

"About a day's hard ride on a fast horse," Emil replied.

"That's not so far," Porthos said hopefully. "How long would it take you to get the army back? A week?"

"A week?" Emil laughed. "It has taken us more than twice that to get here!"

"Surely that's not the fastest the army can move," Catherine put in. "Perhaps if you informed the men that the survival of Paris was at stake . . ."

"This is not a question of my men's motivation," Emil snapped defensively. "We have no horses. The men must march, bearing heavy loads, and many of them do not have the proper shoes. They are doing the best they can."

Greg looked around the camp. "There seem to be at least a few horses."

"Most of them are drays," Emil replied. "They are bred to pull the cannons and the supply carts rather than for speed. Although a few of my officers have faster mounts. I suppose I could get them back to Paris quickly."

"How many would that be?" Aramis asked.

"Thirty, I think."

Greg frowned. A mere thirty extra men wouldn't be much help against an entire army. Plus, he knew how Athos felt about officers in the army: They were almost always members of the upper class who had bought their positions, men who had money but no actual skill. If the Musketeers intended to ride back to confront Condé, it would be nice to bring some actual soldiers along.

Before Greg could figure out how to ask for this diplomatically, however, the crowd parted and the physician arrived.

The man was surprisingly well-to-do compared to most of the others in camp. He wore a far fancier uniform than Emil and had a haughty air about him.

"Monsieur Fallon!" Emil said obsequiously. "Athos here is in grave need of medical attention."

Doctor Fallon glanced down at Athos and frowned with disgust at his swollen leg. "Has anyone taken a urine sample?" he demanded.

"No," Emil admitted.

"Then how am I to make a diagnosis?" Fallon snapped. "Obtain one from him and then I'll be able to tell what is the matter."

Emil nodded obediently and ordered a jar for Athos to urinate in. To Greg's surprise, everyone else seemed quite all right with this.

Greg, however, was beside himself. "You can't tell what the matter is now?" he asked the doctor. "His leg is obviously infected."

"I know that," Fallon replied disdainfully. "But the question is by what? I can't determine that—and the proper treatment—until I analyze his urine."

"Why don't you just examine his leg?" Greg demanded.

Fallon recoiled as though offended. "I am a physician!" he sniffed. "Not some lowly surgeon."

Before Greg could question this logic, Aramis pulled him aside. "I'm not sure how things are done in the future," he said. "But in this time, physicians are far more respected than surgeons. Only men from the upper classes can become physicians. It is regarded as a very cerebral profession. Physicians generally consider that even coming in contact with a patient, let alone touching one, is beneath them. Surgery is considered low-class, as it is manual labor."

"That's insane!" Greg cried. "Surgery takes an incredible amount of skill."

"Really?" Aramis was genuinely surprised. "But it's just cutting."

"Uh, no," Greg countered. "There's a bit more finesse to it than that."

"Not in 1615," Aramis told him.

While all this had been going on, a jar had been procured for Athos, who had managed to urinate in it. The jar was passed to Fallon with great decorum. He held it up to the light and studied its contents carefully.

Given the bright yellow color, Greg could tell that Athos was badly dehydrated—which was hardly a surprise, given how profusely he'd been sweating. Fallon, however, acted as though the jar was full of far more information, the medieval equivalent of an MRI.

"Very interesting," he intoned. "The patient has a severe imbalance of his humors, which has caused the infection. It's irreversible, I'm afraid. The leg will have to come off."

Athos's eyes snapped open in fear, though he was too weak to protest. Emil, Catherine, and the other Musketeers gasped, but Greg couldn't sit by silently.

"Hold on," he challenged. "Imbalance of humors? That doesn't even mean anything!"

Fallon wheeled on him, annoyed. "You dare challenge me? I have a degree in medicine from the University of Paris. What do *you* have?"

"More knowledge than you, apparently," Greg snapped. "You haven't even *asked* what happened to him! He was shot with an arrow. Chances are a piece of it broke off in his leg. That's what's causing the infection. If you cut it out, he'll get better and he can keep the leg."

Greg's friends reacted to this prognosis with excitement, but Fallon was unswayed. "The leg comes off," he said. "Where's the surgeon?"

"Right here," a voice replied. The crowd parted to reveal an unimpressive young man in a bloodied smock. "If you bring him to my tent, I can get started right away."

Before Greg could protest, the soldiers hoisted Athos up and carried him across the field. Greg and the others raced after them. The surgeon's tent was close by. It was merely a canopy set over the grass. There was nothing close to an operating table. The soldiers simply laid Athos on a tarp on the ground. Greg looked around for any sort of surgical tools, but all he saw was a tin cup holding several scissors and razors. The ground was covered with what appeared to be dead grass at first, but as Greg got closer, he realized what it was.

Hair.

"Wait," he said to Aramis. "The surgeon is also the *barber?*"

"Of course," Aramis replied. "All surgeons are. That's why they're called barber-surgeons."

To Greg's horror, the barber-surgeon reached into a small bag and pulled out a rusty old saw. "Oh no," he said. "He can't possibly be thinking about doing the amputation with *that.*"

"What else could get through the bone of the leg?" Aramis asked. "It's very thick."

"No," Greg said. "He can't do this. He'll *kill* Athos."

Aramis nodded gravely. "The survival rate from amputation isn't good." He looked to Greg with great concern. "Do you really think your solution—removing this bit of the arrow—would work?"

"Far better than amputating the leg," Greg said.

"Could you do it?" Aramis asked.

Greg's eyes went wide. "Me? I'm not the surgeon here!"

"No, *he* is." Aramis nodded to the barber-surgeon, who

was spitting on his bone saw to clean it. "Would you prefer *he* operated on Athos?"

Greg gulped. *This is crazy,* he thought. He couldn't possibly operate on his friend. And yet there didn't seem to be any other way to save him. If the surgeon was allowed to amputate, Athos would most likely die—and if by some miracle he lived, he wouldn't be much of a warrior with only one leg. Not in a time where a peg leg was considered the height of prosthetics.

And without Athos, what would the chances be of succeeding against Condé, Milady, and Dinicoeur? Virtually nonexistent. The Musketeers would never have gotten this far without their swordsman.

Before Greg even realized he was doing it, he'd stepped to Athos's side. "Tell that butcher to keep his hands off Athos," he said to the others.

Porthos and Aramis dutifully blocked the surgeon as Greg knelt over Athos, who appeared almost delirious from his fever. "I know you haven't trusted me lately," Greg told his friend. "And I understand why. But you need to trust me now. Because I'm from the future, I know things these men don't. This surgery they're going to perform on you is barbaric, and it will probably kill you. If you'll give me the chance, I can save your life—and maybe even your leg."

Athos's eyes flicked open. He looked to Greg, then to the surgeon, then back to Greg again. For a brief moment, the delirium seemed to fade, as Athos willed himself back to consciousness.

The surgeon was shoving his way past Porthos and Aramis.

"Stop!" Athos yelled, strong enough that everyone froze in their tracks. Athos found Emil and locked eyes with him, then clutched Greg's arm tightly. "My friend here will do whatever it takes to save my leg," he said. "No one else touches me."

And then his eyes rolled back in his head as he lost consciousness.

FIVE

THERE WAS NO ANESTHETIC IN 1615.

A thousand things concerned Greg about performing surgery on Athos, but that was probably the worst. All in all, the operation was going to be rather simple. Greg only needed to locate the bit of arrowhead, tweeze it out, and clean the wound. A doctor in a hospital in the twenty-first century probably could have done it in a minute or two. But without anesthetic, it was going to hurt. A lot.

"There's nothing we can give him?" Greg asked Aramis desperately.

Aramis held up a thin strip of leather, rolled tightly so that it was the width of a finger. "Only this."

"What can that possibly do for him?" Greg asked.

"You put it between his teeth," Aramis explained, "so that when he gnashes them together in pain, he doesn't bite through his own tongue."

Barbaric, Greg thought, shaking his head. *Absolutely barbaric.*

They were in a field. Soldiers loyal to Emil were doing their best to keep the rest of the army at a distance. Greg would have much preferred the privacy of a tent, but the tents were far too dark inside and Greg needed the bright sunlight to operate by. Athos lay on a table before Greg. Some soldiers had procured it from a nearby farmhouse, so Greg wouldn't have to do the operation on his knees. Athos was resting peacefully now. Greg thought his fever might have dropped a bit, but there was no way to know, as thermometers didn't exist yet, either.

They had jury-rigged a set of restraints from their horses' reins and used these to lash Athos's arms and legs down.

The barber-surgeon's "tools" were laid out on the table. To Greg, they looked more like implements of torture than surgical supplies. He'd found them sitting in a cup of bloody water; apparently, the barber-surgeon had no idea that merely rinsing them all in the same cup was a fantastic way to spread disease. At Greg's urging, Porthos and Aramis had washed them as thoroughly as possible, sharpened them on a razor strop, and sterilized them (or at least tried to sterilize them) by heating them over a campfire.

Now the moment of truth had come. Greg couldn't delay it any longer. The sun would set soon, and he needed the full light of day to operate by.

Catherine stood by Athos's side, putting damp rags on his forehead to bring his temperature down and cradling his head in her hands to comfort him. Aramis and Porthos were on hand to help. That was it. Greg had asked the rest of the army to give them privacy; although the soldiers were all gathered not far away, eager to know what was happening.

Greg turned to Aramis. "I guess you should put that thing in his mouth. It's time to start."

Aramis pried Athos's teeth open and set the bit inside. Athos opened his eyes, half-conscious, as though semi-aware that something bad was about to happen.

Greg knelt by Athos to inspect his wound.

It was a quarter-sized hole in Athos's thigh that oozed pus. It went in from the side, into the meatiest part of the muscle, behind the bone. The flesh around it was black and puckered and reeked of infection. "We need to clean this," Greg said. "I need some sterile water."

Aramis had already prepared some ahead of time. He'd heated the water in a tin over the fire until it boiled, then left it to cool. Greg tipped the tin over the wound and poured a tiny bit of the water inside, flushing the pus out.

Athos's eyes went wide and he gritted his teeth on the bit, as if even this had caused him great pain. But he didn't make a sound.

Greg had to repeat the process several times to truly flush the wound. But eventually, the job was done and the wound looked far better already. Unfortunately, Greg had no good way to look inside it. Simple flashlights were still centuries away. The best he could think to do was use the face of his watch to reflect sunlight into the wound.

"Porthos and Aramis, hold him tight," Greg ordered. "Catherine, I need you to hold the wound open."

"Me?" Catherine asked, turning pale.

"You have the most delicate touch of all of us, I think," Greg said. He selected two thin metal rods with fine tips from the surgeon's tools. He shuddered to think what they were actually designed to be used for, but they were the best option he had for the task at hand. "Put these in the hole and pry the sides apart."

Catherine nodded and took the rods. Aramis pinned Athos's arms down while Porthos held his legs. Then Catherine inserted the rods into the wound and gently pried the puckered flesh apart.

Greg was right about her having a delicate touch. Athos bit down again and writhed a bit at the first touch, but the pain seemed to be manageable, and he calmed. "That's great," Greg told her. "In my time, you'd probably make a great doctor."

He then reflected sunlight into the wound. It didn't work very well at all—it was sort of like trying to light a cave with a candle—but after doing it for a minute, he noticed something glint in the wound.

"I think I see it!" he said. He took one of the thin rods and carefully poked at the object, which gave a metallic *clink*. Definitely something that didn't belong in Athos's leg. Greg was able to maneuver it into the meager light.

"I think the whole arrowhead's still in there," he said. "Athos must have just snapped the shaft off instead of trying to pull the whole thing out."

"Well, there was a lot going on at the time," Porthos said, which was quite an understatement. In fact, the boys had been under siege from four assassins with no cover. "I guess he didn't feel he could wait to do it right."

Greg winced, thinking about the pain Athos must have been in all along. *Why hadn't he ever said anything?* he wondered, but he knew the answer. Milady's life and the fate of France had been at stake. Athos would have felt that stopping to care for himself and recuperate would have been self-centered and hardly chivalrous. He probably would have been willing to die for both causes if he had to.

There was only one good thing about the whole arrowhead being in Athos's leg: It'd be that much easier to pull out.

Greg examined the surgical tools, trying to figure out what would work best. He selected a large pair of tweezers—they'd actually come from the army's blacksmith, as they were designed for pulling horseshoe nails out of a horse's hoof—and a pair of thin, sharp scissors that were designed, horrifyingly, for snipping infected tonsils out of the back of a man's throat.

"All right," he warned everyone. "I think this is going to be the rough part."

Aramis cinched the restraints down as tight as they would go. Porthos simply laid his entire bulk across Athos's shins to hold his legs still. Catherine took Greg's watch and held it as close to the wound as she dared to reflect light inside.

Greg poked the tweezers into the wound and tried to pull out the arrowhead.

Now Athos screamed. He roared, despite the bit, and flailed wildly, far more than anyone had expected. Even with his arms and legs lashed, he bucked and writhed.

To make matters worse, the arrowhead didn't come out easily. The only time Greg had ever done something like this before was pulling out thorns and splinters, which came out easily once you got a good grip on them. But the arrowhead had been designed, rather diabolically, to stay where it was. Greg had seen plenty during his time in France. They had little barbs along the edges, like fishhooks, so they would dig into flesh and remain there. There was no choice but to poke the scissors into the wound and snip away around the barbs. Greg was sweating from stress and the heat of the lantern, but he finally managed to clear enough away that he could feel the arrowhead wiggle beneath the scissors.

He stuck the tweezers back in and gave it another try. The arrowhead caught for a moment, then popped free. It was a nasty-looking thing, still sharp after all this time. Thankfully, it was all in one piece, which meant there wasn't anything else back in the wound.

Athos now lay still again, which freed Aramis to come inspect the arrowhead. "Good work," he told Greg. "What do we do now?"

"We need some alcohol," Greg replied.

"For drinking?" Porthos asked.

"It's to sterilize the wound," Greg told him. "This is actually the most important part. We need to kill the infection—or it will kill Athos."

"I'll see what I can do," Porthos said, and then hurried off into camp.

"I think I know something else that may help," Aramis said, and then he ducked away as well.

Greg returned to Athos's side. His friend was unconscious again. The pain of surgery had most likely drained him. He'd bitten almost entirely through the leather bit. "I think we might need another of these," Greg said.

While Catherine dutifully made a second bit, Greg heated the water in the fire again, bringing the temperature back up. Aramis was soon back, his hands full of herbs.

"What's that?" Greg asked.

"Chickweed, plus a few other herbs I saw growing around camp," Aramis replied. "They have healing powers." When Greg frowned skeptically, Aramis said, "They *do*. The church has long documented the effects of these herbs. We're not entirely barbaric in these times."

It occurred to Greg that Aramis probably knew what he was doing far more than the physician had. And his mother was always going on about the healing powers of herbs herself—although she generally took them for headaches, rather than flesh wounds. "All right," Greg said. "Do whatever it takes to make him better."

Aramis quickly prepared a poultice for the wound. He'd just finished when Porthos arrived, clutching a bottle filled with clear alcohol. "Sorry it took so long," he said. "This wasn't easy to get. Apparently, alcohol's worth more than gold to a soldier."

Greg took the bottle. The fumes alone were strong enough to make him dizzy. Whatever this stuff was, it certainly had a lot more alcohol in it than anything his parents drank. Greg figured it would be painful on Athos's raw wound, but unfortunately, he knew of no other way to sterilize it. "Hold him tight," he told the others.

Aramis and Porthos set their weight on Athos's arms and legs again, and when they were ready, Greg carefully poured the alcohol into the wound.

Athos snapped awake again, wailing like a banshee. Catherine knelt over him, stroking his face and doing all she could to calm him. "Everything's all right," she cooed. "It'll all be over soon. Just relax."

Greg dumped the entire bottle into Athos's wound, letting it spill back out again, hopefully flushing out whatever bits of debris and diseased flesh might be left inside. When that was done, he poured in the water he'd heated. While this hurt Athos as well, it was considerably less painful than the alcohol, and he calmed considerably. After Greg had repeated the process several times, the water came out as clear as it had been going in, indicating that the wound was as clean as he was going to get it. He nodded to Aramis, who quickly placed the poultice over the wound and lashed it in place with strips of cloth to protect against any further infection. Aramis's herbal knowledge appeared to be spot-on. No sooner was the poultice on than a look of relief spread across Athos's face and he slipped back into sleep.

Emil rushed over, unable to wait any longer. He had gone white at Athos's final scream and now looked even more disturbed than Athos did. "What's happening?" he demanded. "Is Athos all right?"

"He's fine," Aramis said. "Thanks to D'Artagnan."

Emil's color returned. He turned to Greg, impressed. "Then I owe you a great debt of gratitude."

"We all do," Catherine said. She was looking at Greg now with something more than respect, as though something had changed in how she thought of him. When Greg met her eyes, she turned away, blushing.

The silence was broken by the sound of hoofbeats coming quickly. Greg turned to see the steed gallop into camp and head for the crowd of soldiers. "Where's the commander?" the rider demanded. "I have an urgent message for him."

The soldiers pointed toward Emil. The rider dismounted and rushed over. He was a young boy, barely any older than Greg, and he recoiled with fear upon seeing the makeshift operating room.

"I'm the commander here," Emil said. "What news do you bring?"

"I've just ridden directly from Paris," the messenger replied. "The city is under siege."

SIX

ACCORDING TO THE MESSENGER, CONDÉ'S ARMY HAD begun the siege that very morning. A sentry on the city wall had spotted them just before dawn, coming from the north. King Louis had rallied what few troops he still had, ordered the local farmers to take refuge within the city walls, and dispatched the messenger to find the French army. As he had left before the attack had come, the messenger had no idea what had transpired since, though he guessed Condé's army to number a thousand men.

Emil agreed to turn his army around and start north

toward Paris at first light, although Aramis feared the city wouldn't survive long enough for the soldiers to return. "Not if Milady knows how to breach the city walls," he warned.

And so Aramis, Porthos, Greg, and Catherine decided to ride on ahead of the army. They accepted a hot meal from Emil, as well as new clothes and weapons. They went to bed as soon as the sun went down, intending to catch up on some much-needed sleep, although it seemed to Greg that he had just closed his eyes when Aramis was already shaking him awake. The sky was still dark, so Greg checked his watch.

"It's three in the morning," he protested.

"We've wasted enough time already," Aramis replied. "Paris will not stand for long."

Greg couldn't argue with that. He staggered to his feet and helped Aramis wake Catherine and Porthos.

They had just saddled their horses when a voice caught them by surprise. "Where do you think you're going?"

It was Athos. Greg was stunned to see him awake, let alone out of bed. Athos looked considerably better—the swelling in his leg had gone down dramatically—although he still seemed drained from his ordeal and needed a crutch to support himself.

"Back to Paris," Porthos replied, and quickly filled Athos in on what had happened.

"Then I'm coming with you," Athos replied.

"No," Aramis said. "You need to rest. You almost died because you wouldn't take care of yourself before."

"And now, thanks to D'Artagnan, I'm fixed." Athos flashed a smile, looking more like his old self than he had in days. "I'm not going to sit here twiddling my thumbs while the rest of you run off to confront Dinicoeur and Milady and Condé. Without me, you'll all be dead in five minutes."

"No," Aramis repeated. "You might feel better, but you're not. Not yet. We'll be all right without you."

"You won't even be able to get back into the city without me," Athos replied.

The others looked at him curiously. "What do you mean?" Porthos asked.

"You can't simply walk up to the city gates in the middle of a siege and ask to be allowed in," Athos explained. "The moment anyone opens the gates, the enemy will sweep in. That means you'll need to use the secret entrances, but you don't know where they are, do you?"

Greg frowned in response. The truth was, the map he'd seen had only indicated the approximate locations of the three secret entrances to the city. Finding them, however, certainly wouldn't be easy. "And you do?" he asked.

"I know one," Athos replied smugly. "I learned it when I was in the king's guard. Unfortunately, it's almost impossible to describe where the entrance is. So I'll just have to show you."

Greg wondered whether this was true. He suspected that

Athos certainly could have described the entrance's location and was merely pretending otherwise so he'd be asked to come along.

Aramis, Porthos, and Catherine leaned in closely to Greg. "Could he truly be ready to travel so soon?" Aramis asked.

"I suppose," Greg replied. "I'm not a doctor or anything, but his wound wasn't really that big. It was the infection that was killing him. And if we took care of that, I suppose he could recover quickly. I'd probably want to spend another few days in bed, but this is Athos we're talking about." He pointed toward Athos, who was currently practicing how to sword-fight while using a crutch at the same time. "He certainly seems to be feeling better."

Catherine smiled and shook her head in amazement. "Far better than he would if they'd sawed off his leg."

Aramis approached Athos again. "All right," he said. "You can come with us. But promise me, if the exertion starts to make you worse again, you'll stop. You're worth far more to us alive than dead."

"I won't be slowing anyone down," Athos said. "If anything, you'll be slowing *me*." With that, he clambered on one of the horses and spurred it on.

The others raced to their horses and followed. They galloped after Athos, through the camp, and onto the Roman road again, heading north toward Paris.

As he'd threatened, Athos set the pace, riding hard the whole way. Greg suspected that his friend's leg was still in great pain, but the swordsman didn't show it. He didn't put any weight on it if he could help it, but other than that, he rode as fast as any of the others. After a few hours, Greg felt as though *he* was the one who'd been operated on. His muscles burned and he was dizzy with fatigue. But still, they pressed on.

They reached Paris just before noon and found it in the midst of a full-on siege.

Condé's army might have been smaller than Richelieu's, but it had come prepared with siege weapons. Greg could count a dozen catapults and trebuchets, one of which launched a huge rock at the city walls while he watched. The rock smashed into the ramparts, scattering the guards there and shattering a merlon as though it were made of glass. The huge weapons allowed the army to attack from afar, keeping out of range of any arrows the Parisians could fire. While Condé had the city surrounded, the bulk of his attack was focused on the eastern side. Until a few months before, this side of the city had been protected by the Bastille, a large fortress, but Michel Dinicoeur had badly damaged that when he'd freed Dominic Richelieu from its dungeon, and it had yet to be fully repaired. The city wall was weakened there, and now Condé's army was building a massive battering ram, apparently hoping to destroy the fortifications once and for all.

Fortunately, the secret entrance Athos knew of began far beyond enemy lines. "It's an abandoned limestone mine," he explained.

"Like the one the Spanish assassin chased D'Artagnan into?" Porthos asked.

"Yes," Athos replied. "From what I understand, there are several abandoned mines around Paris. The difference is, this one actually runs *underneath* the city. It was built hundreds of years ago—I've heard that most of the stone for Notre Dame came from it. But it's long been forgotten."

Athos led the others to one of the few bits of forest still standing near Paris, two acres of trees atop a rocky mound that every farmer knew was impossible to clear and plow. They left their horses at the edge and pushed into the woods on foot. To Greg's surprise, Athos seemed even better after the long ride than he had before it, as though the exercise had done him good. His fever appeared to be gone, and while he still limped to keep his full weight off his wounded leg, he was barely even using the crutch. He led the way through the woods so quickly, it was difficult to keep up.

Still, it took him a while to locate the entrance. It was hidden deep in a tangle of underbrush, near the base of an ancient oak tree that looked like a hundred others nearby.

The only difference was that at the base of this one, there was a hole between two of the roots. The hole wasn't even that big, barely wide enough for a man to wriggle through. "This is it," Athos said.

"That?" Porthos asked. "That little thing is the secret entrance to Paris?"

"Well, if it were a giant tunnel with signs all around it saying, 'This way to Paris,' it wouldn't be much of a secret, would it?" Athos shot back.

"I know that," Porthos said, then glanced down at his large belly. "I just expected something that I could actually, well . . . fit through."

"It's only the entrance that's this tight," Athos told him. "In order to keep it hidden. It widens out inside."

"How much?" Catherine asked. Though she could easily fit through the entrance, Greg noticed that she didn't look very eager to head down through the narrow, muddy hole.

"A bit," Athos said, though without much confidence. He stooped to wriggle into the tunnel, but before anyone could take another step, he held up his hand. He knelt by the mine entrance and inspected the muddy ground there. "Someone else has been through here," he said.

Greg and the others leaned in to see that there were two sets of boot prints in the mud. They appeared to be exactly the same size.

"Dinicoeur and Richelieu," Aramis said.

"Are you sure?" Catherine asked, now looking even more worried.

"No," Aramis replied. "But what other two men with the same size feet would have come this way? Dinicoeur knows all the secret entrances into the city—and we already suspected he would be returning to Paris." He turned to Athos. "Can you tell how long ago the prints were made?"

Athos pressed a finger into the mud. "I can't say for sure, but since this mud's still wet, they seem quite fresh. I'd guess it hasn't been too long. Less than a few hours, if that."

"Then we don't have a moment to lose," Aramis said. "Lead the way."

Athos nodded and started into the tunnel again.

"Wait!" Porthos called out.

Athos swung back toward him. "What now?"

"Isn't anyone else bothered by the fact that our enemies just came through here?" Porthos asked. "What if they're waiting in the cave to ambush us in there?"

"I don't think that's likely," Aramis explained. "In the first place, it's not so surprising that Dinicoeur and Richelieu came this way. There are only three secret entrances into the city, and this is the only one on the southern side. To use any of the others, they'd have to circle around past Condé's army. They've merely done what we did: get to the closest access point. If anything, we should be pleased to learn they came through recently. It means that we've nearly caught up to them."

"And the ambush . . . ?" Porthos asked.

"They probably think we're dead," Aramis said. "I'm sure they heard that we'd been captured by Condé and sent to Les Baux. Condé wanted the entire countryside to know that."

"We don't know that they heard that news for sure, though," Greg cautioned. "And even if Dinicoeur and Richelieu knew we'd been captured, that doesn't mean they wouldn't be prepared for us anyway."

"Still," Aramis said, "they couldn't possibly know that we're trailing so closely behind them or that we'd follow them here. They're not going to be waiting in the tunnel to attack us."

"Probably not," Greg admitted. "But they could have booby-trapped it, just to be on the safe side. They'd certainly know that if we *did* return to Paris, we'd most likely use this tunnel. And for that matter, Milady also knows this route exists. I wouldn't put it past her to leave a surprise for us—or Dinicoeur."

Porthos gulped. "Maybe we ought to try a different entrance then."

"We can't," Athos grumbled. "This is the only one I know the exact location of. And even if I did know where the others were, we wouldn't have the time to get to them."

Porthos frowned. "All right," he said. "I guess we have to go this way. But I think D'Artagnan's right. We need to be very cautious."

"And yet we need to move as quickly as possible," Athos said, with a glance at Aramis.

"Er, yes," Aramis admitted.

"I'll see what I can do," Athos said with a sigh. And then he slipped into the tunnel.

Porthos went next. As he'd feared, he barely made it through the opening. For a moment, he actually got wedged in the hole, but then he sucked in his belly and squeezed through.

Greg went next, with Catherine and Aramis close behind him.

Inside, the tunnel was damp, claustrophobic, and pitch-black. After going only a few steps, Greg couldn't see an inch in front of his face. It was extremely unnerving—especially knowing that Dinicoeur or Milady might have left a trap. He was sorely tempted to use his last remaining match to light a torch, but he felt he needed to save it for a true emergency. Besides, the tunnel was so cramped, it would have been impossible to carry a live flame. At several points, everyone had to get on their hands and knees to wriggle through a narrow spot.

To find the way through in the darkness, Athos followed a series of markings that had been carved into the wall, sort of like signposts for the blind. There were several tunnels that branched off the main one, and Athos cautioned everyone to stay close together and not make a wrong turn. "It's a maze down here," he warned. "If someone ends up going the wrong way in the dark, there's a decent chance they'll never find their way out again."

"What's our priority when we get to the city?" Porthos asked. "Do we try to track down Dinicoeur first? Or Milady? Or find the other half of this Devil's Stone?"

"I'd say we find Milady," Athos suggested. "She's the biggest threat right now. She's had the biggest head start on us, and unlike Dinicoeur and Richelieu, the king doesn't know not to trust her. He has no idea she's in league with Condé. As long as she's around, Louis is in grave danger."

"I agree," Aramis said. "Plus, Dinicoeur will be looking for Milady himself. She has half the Devil's Stone—and he needs it to get the second half."

Plus, she has my phone, Greg thought.

"So if we find Milady, we'll probably find Dinicoeur close by?" Catherine asked.

"I'd assume so," Aramis said. "There's not much he can do without the stone."

"Is that right, D'Artagnan?" Porthos asked.

"I suppose," Greg replied. "I don't really know any more about him than Aramis does."

"Really?" Athos asked. "I thought he was your direct ancestor. Your great-great-great-great-grandfather or something like that."

"Yes, but I didn't know that until recently," Greg admitted. "You have to go a long way back in my family until you get to him."

"Oh my." Porthos stopped so suddenly that Greg slammed into him. "I just realized something. I'd been thinking that the best way to defeat Dinicoeur is to kill Richelieu. . . ."

"It *is*," Athos said. "If we kill Richelieu before he becomes immortal, then that negates Dinicoeur's existence, right? Dinicoeur can't exist if Richelieu doesn't exist to become him."

"I think that's how it works," Aramis agreed.

"But if we do that, won't we negate D'Artagnan's existence, too?" Porthos asked. "If Richelieu dies before he has a child, then no one in D'Artagnan's family will ever exist."

There was a moment of chilling silence in the darkness. "I'd never thought of that," Athos said.

"That might not be an issue," Catherine told the others. "Richelieu already has a son."

"He does?" Porthos asked.

"It's not common knowledge," Catherine said. "Richelieu tries to keep it a secret. I rarely heard him mention the boy in all the time I worked in his quarters. He's not married to the mother, and I don't think he sees the child very often."

"How old is the boy?" Porthos asked.

"Only a few months," Catherine replied.

"Is his name Stefan?" Greg asked.

"Yes," Catherine told him. "Is that your ancestor?"

"Yes," Greg said. That was the name his great-great-grandfather had given in the diary Greg had found. And yet he didn't feel any relief from this discovery. Instead, he felt even more unsettled. Now that he knew how devious and desperate Michel Dinicoeur was, he had a horrifying idea about what the man might be plotting now.

"Ah," Porthos said cheerily. "Well, that's settled then. Your ancestor exists, D'Artagnan. Sorry if I got you all worked up. There's nothing to worry about."

"Actually, there *is*," Greg said. "What would happen if Stefan died before *he* had children?"

There was another silence, even more chilling than the first. "Oh no," Catherine said. "Dinicoeur would continue to exist—but *you* wouldn't."

"And if D'Artagnan didn't exist, that would alter *our* history," Aramis said. "We're only together now because he brought us together. Without him, there might not even be any Musketeers. . . ."

"Which means there'd be no one to stop Dinicoeur," Athos finished.

"Do you think he could be so diabolical?" Catherine asked. "To do something to his own son just to protect himself . . ."

"Nothing is too diabolical for Dinicoeur," Greg told her. "Do you have any idea where his son lives?"

"Not exactly," Catherine admitted. "But I know the part of town and the mother's name."

"Then take us there," Athos said. "Milady is no longer our priority. Protecting that child is. We must move faster. There is no time to waste!"

SEVEN

Dominic Richelieu followed his future self quickly through the streets of Paris.

Michel was moving with surprising speed, given that he had seemed to be at death's door a few days earlier. He hadn't healed completely, of course; his skin was still cracked and burnt, and there wasn't a hair left on his body. This was all easy to hide, however. Michel wore a shawl draped over his head and wrapped around his arms, hiding every bit of skin. He looked no different from the hundreds of poor beggars who lurked in the alleys of Paris. No one gave him a second glance—although with the city under siege, everybody was distracted more than usual. Michel had a leather bag slung around his neck, in which he carried several diabolical things he'd made with his knowledge from the future: some poisons, chloroform, and a cluster of grenades. Though heavy, it didn't slow him down. Michel just lurched along through the crowds, driven by his new plan, moving so fast that Dominic had trouble keeping up.

In truth, Dominic found Michel's amazing recovery unsettling—but then, virtually everything about Michel was unsettling. Dominic now realized that in some way, he'd been in a state of shock ever since meeting the man who claimed to be his four-hundred-year-old self from the future. Who wouldn't have felt that way? Since Michel's arrival a few months before, much of Dominic's life had seemed a bizarre dream.

And yet the last week had been the most bizarre of all. After his defeat on the Pont du Gard, Michel had changed. Up until that point, Dominic had gotten along famously with his older self. Perhaps that shouldn't have been a surprise, as they were technically the same person—but as far as Dominic was concerned, they weren't the same at all. Michel had lived a tremendously long life, learned a staggering number of things, and experienced a horrible amount of suffering. Those things all changed a man. To Dominic, Michel was more like a wise and distant ancestor. All they really had in common was their looks—and their desire for power.

Thus, Dominic had been happy to listen to Michel's plans for how to obtain that power. After all, the whole reason Michel had come back was to help *him*. If everything went well, he would get the eternal life of wealth and privilege that Michel had long ago dreamed of for himself. And when that happened, Michel would most likely vanish like a dream.

But things hadn't worked out as Michel had planned.

The first time they'd been defeated by the Musketeers, he'd weathered things well. He'd been angry, of course, but he'd quickly hatched a plan that would have given them even more power than he'd originally thought possible: complete control of France.

Once the Musketeers had defeated them the second time, however, leaving Michel burnt and broken, things had changed. Ever since, Michel had been consumed with fury. He had been curt and testy with Dominic—as if *Dominic* was somehow responsible for everything going wrong at the aqueduct. And now, for the first time, Dominic knew Michel was keeping something from him. Before, Michel had always been completely open about what his plans were—in fact, he had gleefully discussed every detail with Dominic. But now he was keeping much to himself. Dominic had repeatedly pressed him for more information during their ride north to Paris, but Michel had remained stubbornly silent the entire way.

"Could you at least tell me where we are going?" Dominic asked now.

"Now? Surrounded by all these people? Are you an idiot?" Michel snapped. "You'll find out soon enough. If you spent more time following orders and less time questioning them, we'd be there already."

"I'm not some subordinate you can just boss around," Dominic shot back. "We're in this together, you and I."

"I'm well aware of that," Michel replied. "Everything I'm doing now—everything I've *ever* done—has been done for you. So why don't you just trust me and do as I say?"

Dominic felt like snapping back, saying that he'd trusted Michel plenty and it hadn't ever worked out as well as promised—but he held his tongue. There was no point to arguing. It would only draw attention. And if anyone took a real hard look at Michel, they'd be terrified by what they saw. The people of Paris were on edge as it was. If they suddenly found a walking corpse in their midst, they'd probably try to stone him to death.

Suddenly something whistled through the air. Dominic spun toward the sound and saw all the Parisians either pointing toward the city wall or running away from it. A huge stone, launched from one of Condé's catapults, sailed into the city and smashed into the steeple of a small church. The rock took a massive bite out of the steeple and crashed to earth, the steeple toppling in its wake.

While the townspeople cried in despair and alarm,

Michel barely gave the damage a glance. He just kept on going, headed for the Seine, focused only on his plan.

Condé, Dominic thought. That was something else Michel hadn't seen coming. When Dominic had been scouring the countryside around the Pont du Gard for food and horses, he had pieced together the story of what had happened. How Milady—whom Michel had always dismissed as a mere strumpet—had teamed up with Condé, betrayed the Musketeers, and sent them to their deaths in Les Baux. Even that news hadn't made a dent in Michel's anger, however.

"I won't believe they're dead until I kill them all myself" was how he'd responded.

They turned onto the Pont Neuf to cross to the north side of the Seine, but once they reached the point where the bridge intersected with the Île de la Cité, Michel turned off and headed east across the island.

"We're not heading to the palace?" Dominic asked.

"Not yet," Michel replied.

"But I thought you said Milady would return to the palace. And she has one half of the Devil's Stone."

"Which we will get in due time."

"Are we going for the other half then? The one that is hidden—"

"The stone is not our major concern at this moment."

"But if it is the key to making me immortal again—"

"Just stop asking questions and do as I tell you," Michel

barked. "Everything will work out soon enough."

Dominic sullenly fell silent again. But then Michel turned north onto another bridge. One that Dominic knew very well. "Michel, this is where—"

Michel suddenly stopped and swung around to face him. His eyes blazed from beneath the folds of his cloak, boring into Dominic's. They were so close, Dominic got a strong whiff of his future self, and the odor took him aback. Michel still smelled a bit like burnt flesh—but there was something worse mixed in there. Death. He reeked of death.

"Stay here," Michel ordered. "Find a place where you won't stand out. I'll be back soon."

"And what am I supposed to do?"

"Keep an eye out. If any of the Musketeers comes along"—Michel tapped the sword tucked into Dominic's belt—"take care of them."

"The Musketeers?" Dominic laughed. "They're probably swinging from the gallows in Les Baux by now."

"I have underestimated the Musketeers one time too many," Michel growled. "I do not intend to take any more chances where they are concerned. Not until I have taken care of them once and for all."

"What do you mean?"

"You'll understand soon enough. Just stay here and do as I said." Michel started toward the bridge, then stopped and turned back once more. "But do not do anything foolish, either. If only one Musketeer comes along, kill him. If, somehow, all of them have survived, stand down and come find me. I'd hate to go through all this trouble to make you immortal, only to have you die now."

Dominic nodded, understanding, and Michel turned away again. He fell in with the flow of people passing over the bridge. No one noticed the burnt and scarred immortal man in their midst.

Dominic found a spot across the road from the bridge. There was a narrow alley, and he melted into the shadow of it. His mission seemed ridiculous. Even if the Musketeers had survived everything, how could they possibly end up here? Dominic himself hadn't even known they would be coming this way. And yet Michel had a point. Time and time again, the Musketeers had surprised them.

So Dominic readied his sword and kept an eye out, all the while wondering what Michel was up to.

EIGHT

THE TUNNEL SEEMED TO GO ON FOREVER. THE TRIP through the long, dank, claustrophobic shaft would have been terrible under normal circumstances, but now, knowing that every second counted, the trip was agonizing. Just when Greg thought he might go mad from being in the darkness, a shaft of light appeared ahead. It peeked around the frame of a door at the end of the tunnel.

Athos pushed it open, and the Musketeers emerged to find themselves in the crypt of a small cathedral. Ahead, an eerie narrow passage was lined with walls of ancient human bones that had been stacked like firewood and studded with skulls in intricate patterns.

"What's the point of all this?" Greg gasped.

"This isn't done in the future?" Aramis asked. "What happens to your dead?"

"We bury them," Greg replied.

"Oh," Aramis said, sounding disappointed that the answer wasn't something more amazing. "We do that, too—outside the city. But within the walls, the cemeteries ran out of space long ago—and most of the poor can't afford a burial anyhow. So the bones end up here, in these abandoned mines."

"I kind of like it," Catherine said. "I'd rather end up as part of a piece of art than merely rotting in a box in the earth somewhere."

Greg saw her point, although it didn't make the passage through the tunnel of bones any less disquieting. Still, he had to admit that it was infinitely better than the claustrophobic old mine had been.

"Look!" Porthos knelt on the floor. There were two sets of footprints, wet from the damp in the tunnel. "The water hasn't even had time to evaporate yet. That means Dinicoeur and Richelieu must be only a few minutes ahead of us."

The boys and Catherine hurried up the stairs and into the cathedral. It was much smaller than Notre Dame, but it was still a beautiful edifice; the stone for it had come directly from its own basement. The church bell clanged once, high above their heads. One p.m.

"I know this place!" Aramis cried. "It is Saint John the Divine! We're on the south side of the city, near the garment district."

"Richelieu's son lives close by," Catherine said. "Near Saint-Germain."

Everyone raced out the door and into Paris. Greg was instantly aware that the city had changed greatly in his absence; the siege had already taken its toll. And yet he was in such a hurry, he couldn't even take the time to look around. He only caught glimpses as he ran: streets that seemed far more crowded than before, now that the rural families from the surrounding area had been forced to take refuge within the city; heavily armed soldiers posted all along the ramparts; a church steeple that lay in ruins, shattered by a massive rock that had been catapulted over the wall.

Greg's parents were somewhere out there. He desperately wanted to find them, to hug them tightly and tell them how much he'd missed them, but there was no time. If he didn't act quickly, they—and he himself—would cease to exist at all.

The team arrived in a poor neighborhood wedged between the wall of the Saint-Germain monastery and the Seine River, full of ramshackle homes and narrow, twisting alleys. "This is the place," Catherine announced.

"How do we find the right home in all this?" Greg asked desperately.

"How else?" Aramis replied. To answer his own question, he pointed at the local church. It was a modest building, not much bigger than some of the nearby homes. Aramis pushed through the door.

A young priest looked up from the altar, surprised at the intrusion. "May I help you?"

"We're looking for a woman who lives in this neighborhood," Aramis told him. "Her life is in grave danger."

"Her name is Teresa," Catherine added. "She is unwed, but she has a young son named Stefan."

The priest's eyes lit up. "Ah, yes! I know Teresa well. She used to live just down the street. But sadly, she couldn't pay her rent and was evicted. What sort of trouble is she in? Is it something I can help with?"

"Hopefully, we can get to her before she needs you," Athos replied. "Do you know where she moved to?"

"She has a sister," the priest said. "She and her husband live on the Bridge of Saint Denis, by the Place de Grève. They have a cheese shop on the first floor. I believe Teresa has gone to live there. . . ."

The Musketeers were out the door before he could finish. As they ran toward the bridge, however, Greg saw the others were beginning to flag. Athos, normally the fastest, had already put far too much strain on his wounded leg. He was pushing himself as hard as he could, but he just couldn't go as quickly as usual. Meanwhile, the others were simply falling behind, winded from the exertion. Greg knew he should be exhausted himself, but he didn't feel it. The knowledge that his own fate—and that of everyone in his entire family—hung in the balance drove him onward. He didn't want to face Dinicoeur and Richelieu alone, but he couldn't wait for the others, either. Right now, every second counted.

He pushed ahead, although the others implored him not to.

"D'Artagnan, wait!" Catherine cried.

"You're no match for the two of them by yourself!" Athos warned.

"I'll be all right!" Greg yelled back to them. "Just get to Teresa's as fast as you can!"

Although Paris was one of the largest cities in Europe in 1615, it was still surprisingly small compared to any major city in the twenty-first century. Greg knew from experience that he could run from one side to the other in a little more than ten minutes.

He had learned the city well during his time there; Athos had taught him the fastest ways to get from place to place. The city was split by the Seine, with the Île de la Cité—the island that Notre Dame sat on—at the very center. The Louvre palace sat on the northern bank of the Seine at the western edge of the city, while the Bastille fortress mirrored it on the east. Between them was a maze of narrow alleys and twisting streets, lined with hovels, shops, churches, and the occasional mansion.

Greg raced from southern Paris over the first bridge across the Seine, then across the Île de la Cité, until he arrived at the Bridge of Saint Denis. It was one of several bridges in Paris that had homes built along the sides, as if it were merely another road. (There was little space within the city walls, and homes were built wherever anyone could find space.) As the bridge was close to the city's central market, Place de Grève, most homes had a shop on the first floor and living quarters above. Unfortunately, many of these shops sold cheese; there seemed to be at least a dozen. Greg stood in the middle of the bridge for a moment, glancing from one to the other, wondering which—if any—was the one where Teresa now lived.

And then he noticed that only one shop had no one working at the counter. He rushed over. Behind the small wooden rack where freshly made cheeses were displayed, a stout woman lay sprawled on the floor. Behind her, in the shadows, her husband was laid out beside an overturned churn.

Greg feared they were dead, but then saw a rag lying close to the woman's head. It gave off a faint chemical smell. *Chloroform.*

Only one person in 1615 knew how to make chloroform. Michel Dinicoeur was already here.

Greg unsheathed his sword and nervously glanced

around the cheese shop. In the far corner, he spotted the narrow staircase that led upstairs.

There was a small window next to it, allowing a view of the Seine River. Greg caught a glimpse of his reflection in it—and saw something moving quickly behind him.

He leaped to the side just as the sword sliced through the air. It barely missed Greg and slammed down so hard, it cleaved an entire wheel of cheese in two.

Greg spun around and saw that his attacker was none other than Dominic Richelieu. He raised his own sword as Richelieu attacked again, and parried.

A scream rang out from the room above.

Greg raced for the staircase, knowing that there would be no other way out from upstairs—that he was racing into a dead end—and yet there was nothing else he could do. He was sure that he had only seconds, if that, to act.

Richelieu came after him.

Greg pounded up the stairs and burst into the living quarters. There was only one room, which served as kitchen, dining room, bedroom, and nursery. Dinicoeur was there, although his back was to Greg, so the person Greg really noticed was Teresa.

She was very young and beautiful, and Greg instantly knew she had to be related to him. Despite the fact that there were a dozen generations between them, he could see she had his mother's eyes. And yet there was something more, a strange sense of connection he could feel. Teresa was wailing, partly in fear and partly in despair, reaching toward Dinicoeur, who now spun toward Greg.

Greg staggered back at the sight of him.

The man was now a monster. His face was a mask of charred flesh. His hair was gone, and his burnt lips were twisted into a horrible sneer. He'd have been unrecognizable if it hadn't been for his eyes. They were still the same, blazing with anger and hate.

A baby, less than a year old, was wailing in his arms.

Greg was so stunned by the sight of Dinicoeur and Stefan, he nearly forgot about Richelieu. He sprang away from the top of the stairs at the last instant as Richelieu charged through, swinging his blade.

"Dominic!" Teresa called, actually relieved to see him, as though he could only be here to save her. "Help us!"

Dominic froze, his sword in the air, and spun toward her. Greg saw his face fill with several emotions at once. He seemed excited to see his son again, but startled to see the infant in Michel's hands. More than anything, however, he appeared confused, and Greg instantly understood. *He doesn't know what Michel is doing,* he thought. *Michel hasn't told him.* Dinicoeur's plan was so diabolical he hadn't even revealed it to his own younger self. Now, Richelieu merely stared, trying to make sense of what he was seeing.

"Get him!" Dinicoeur yelled, and Richelieu snapped out of his daze and obediently slashed at Greg again.

Greg met Richelieu's sword with his own. "Dominic!" he

yelled. "Michel is killing your son!"

Dominic continued to attack—but he now seemed somewhat hesitant about it.

Greg realized what the problem was: There was more Dinicoeur hadn't told his younger self. "I'm your descendant!" he yelled, ducking as Dominic slashed at him. "Michel is trying to make sure I never existed!"

Richelieu froze in mid-attack as understanding broke through. Then he wheeled back toward Dinicoeur. "No!!!" he roared. "Give the boy to me!"

Dinicoeur backed away, raising his sword to his younger self. "I'm doing this for *us*, you fool!" he snarled.

"You're doing it for *you*!" Richelieu cried. "I would *never* have agreed to this!"

Now that Dinicoeur was distracted by his younger self, Teresa grabbed the fireplace poker and clobbered him so hard that he staggered into the wall. Stefan tumbled from his grasp, but Teresa snatched the infant before he hit the ground.

Dinicoeur bellowed in rage and backhanded Teresa across the face. She tumbled backward, clutching Stefan. Greg caught both of them, and they all crashed to the floor.

Stefan was safe, however. The infant howled, and as he did, Dinicoeur advanced on them, his sword glinting in the lamplight. However, Richelieu caught his arm and held him back. "No!" he said. "There must be another way!"

Greg snatched his sword off the floor, ready to defend Stefan with his life.

"D'Artagnan!" A cry came from the street below. Athos. "Where are you?"

"Up here!" Greg yelled back. "Hurry!"

More voices carried from the street. The other Musketeers.

"Hold on!" Aramis yelled.

"We're coming!" Porthos cried.

Dinicoeur hissed in anger, then allowed Richelieu to pull him away. They ducked down the staircase, fleeing before the Musketeers could arrive.

Greg heaved a sigh of relief. He looked down at the wailing baby in his arms. It was bizarre: He was holding his own ancestor. And yet there was also something rejuvenating about it. Holding Stefan seemed to fill him with life and energy.

He felt the same sensation coming from Teresa as well. He turned to face her, to explain everything, but she wasn't looking at him. Her eyes were riveted on something else just beyond him. "What is *that*?" she gasped.

Greg spun around and saw something the size and shape of an orange. Two curved metal pieces had been welded together to make a ball, from which a wick protruded. The wick was lit, sparking with fire.

"It's a grenade!" Greg exclaimed.

Dinicoeur might have left with Richelieu, but he hadn't

listened to the pleas from his younger self to let Stefan live. The grenade sat between Greg and the stairs. The wick had almost burned up. Greg figured he had only a few seconds left at best.

There wasn't enough time to get Stefan and Teresa out of the house.

NINE

THERE WAS ONLY ONE THING GREG COULD DO.

"Cover Stefan!" he told Teresa. "And get down!"

He shoved the infant into Teresa's arms, dashed across the room, snatched the grenade off the floor, and heaved it out the window toward the Seine.

The bomb might have been small, but it was much heavier than he'd expected. The thing felt like it was almost solid metal. After smashing through the glass, it barely cleared the windowsill.

Greg spun around just as the grenade exploded.

There was a flash of orange light. Greg caught a glimpse of Teresa, curled in a ball around Stefan on the floor—and then the concussion of air sent him flying.

The house shuddered from the blast. The window shattered inward and hot shards of glass rained down. Greg tumbled across the floor and slammed into the wall.

He lay there for a moment, eyes shut tight, ears ringing from the explosion, until he felt it was safe to take a look around again.

The first thing he saw was Teresa. She appeared terrified, but otherwise unscathed. In her arms, Stefan was wailing.

Greg scrambled to the infant's side and looked him over. He didn't have a scratch on him, thanks to his mother; he was only crying due to fright.

The grenade had blown out almost the entire side of the house and part of the floor as well. A few licks of flame danced around the edges of the hole. Through it, Greg could see straight down the Seine. Parisians were gathered all along the riverbanks, staring at the house in astonishment. There were quite a few startled fishermen in boats on the river, but thankfully, no one had been hurt.

Greg realized Teresa was staring at him. He turned back to her and looked into the wide brown eyes. "Who are you?" she asked.

"I'm a, uh . . . a very distant relative of yours," Greg replied.

"Why did that . . . that *thing* want to kill my son?"

"It's a little hard to explain," Greg said. "Are you all right?"

"Yes," Teresa said. "Stefan and I both are, I think."

"Then we ought to get out of here just in case this whole place comes down." Greg warily eyed the fire flickering around the hole in the wall.

Teresa held out her hand, and Greg helped her to her feet. The staircase hadn't been damaged in the blast, and they hurried down it and through the cheese shop.

There was a large crowd gathered outside. The moment Greg emerged into the daylight, he was mobbed by people, demanding to know what had happened. To Greg's relief, the Musketeers pushed through the crowd along with Catherine, who flung her arms around him and held him tightly. "Are you all right?" she asked.

"I'm fine," Greg said. "And I'm going to stay that way, now that Stefan is okay." He turned to Teresa. "Teresa, these are the Musketeers. They're here to help you."

Teresa's eyes widened. "The Musketeers? But I'd heard you all were fighting the Spanish in the south."

"We defeated them," Aramis told her. "So now we've returned."

Teresa frowned as she thought back to the events that had just happened. "To get the man who was with Dominic?"

"Yes," Greg replied, and then turned to the others. "What happened to Dinicoeur and Richelieu?"

Athos shrugged apologetically. "They got away. We saw them run out of the building, but then the explosion happened. Everyone in the streets panicked and ran. It was chaos, and Dinicoeur and Richelieu took advantage of it to cover their escape."

"Then this isn't over," Greg said. "We need to find a place where Teresa and Stefan will be safe."

"Notre Dame," Aramis suggested. "All who are in need are welcome there."

Greg shook his head. "Dinicoeur will think of that. In fact, he'll probably canvass every church in town."

"I know a place he'll never find them," Porthos said. "The home of a good friend. It has a secret room in the cellar."

"Let's take them there now," Greg said. He started through the crowd, but Athos caught his arm.

"I'm afraid there isn't time for all of us to do that," Athos said. "Right now, there are so many urgent issues, I think we have no choice but to split up. Porthos can see Teresa and Stefan to safety himself. Meanwhile, we still have Milady and Condé to deal with." Athos pointed to Greg. "You and Catherine go to the palace. Tell the king all that has happened and let him know his life is in danger. There's a good chance Condé's assassins are already within the city."

"Then shouldn't *you* come?" Greg asked. "You're the best swordsman of us all."

"Not anymore," Athos said. "My leg is still not fully

healed. Now *you're* the best swordsman of us all. Protect Louis. Meanwhile, I'm going to see about getting those secret entrances to the city sealed off."

"By yourself?" Porthos asked.

"No," Athos told him. "I still have some friends in the king's guard. I'm sure I can get some help."

"But we don't even know where all the entrances are," Aramis protested.

"Yes we do." Athos reached into his cloak and pulled out a folded piece of paper. "Emil wrote this up for me last night. As a commander of the army, he's one of the few people who knows all their locations. He gave it to me this morning, before we left."

"That's still a big job," Aramis said. "I could help with that."

"No," Athos said. "You need to figure out where in this city the Devil's Stone is hidden. Sooner or later, Milady or Dinicoeur is going to come looking for it, and we need to beat them there. For all we know, that's where Dinicoeur is now."

"But the city is huge!" Aramis protested. "The stone could be anywhere in it."

"That's why you'd better get started looking," Athos said. "Start with the library at Notre Dame. If anyone can determine where the stone—or this Crown of Minerva—is, it's you." Athos turned to the others. "Let's use Notre Dame as our base. If we need to find each other, we go there."

Greg didn't like the idea of splitting up, but Athos was right. There was too much to do.

Porthos held his hand out. "One for all," he said.

The others placed their hands atop his. "And all for one," they chimed.

Then they went their separate ways. Greg took only a few steps toward the Louvre, however, then turned back to watch the others: Porthos hurrying north with Teresa and Stefan, Athos heading east toward the city wall, and Aramis moving south toward Notre Dame.

"What's bothering you?" Catherine asked.

"This just seems wrong somehow," Greg told her. "The four of us haven't been apart for over a month—and we've been through so much in that time."

"You'll see them again soon," Catherine said.

"I think that's just it," Greg said. "I'm worried that I *won't* see them. Without the others around, no one has our backs."

"They'll be all right." Catherine slipped her hand into Greg's and gave it a reassuring squeeze.

Greg turned to face her. At least he wasn't alone, he thought. "You're right. They will," he said, although he didn't really believe that. There were still too many enemies on the loose. He couldn't shake the nagging fear that this might have been the last time he saw all the Musketeers alive.

"Then come on." Catherine tugged on Greg's hand, and

he obediently turned and followed her toward the palace.

Catherine kept her hand in Greg's as they hurried through the city. It was only a short distance from Saint Denis to the palace—less than ten blocks. She was silent for the first half of it, though Greg could tell there was something on her mind. Finally, she said, "Actually, I'm sort of glad it's just you and me for once."

"Really?" Greg said. "Why?"

"Well, with all that's happened, you and I haven't been alone together since Arles. And there's something I wanted to talk to you about." Catherine turned to Greg, then grew embarrassed and turned away again. "It seems so improper of me to say this, but you've said that in the future, women aren't so bound by convention."

"I can't imagine you ever doing anything improper," Greg said.

Catherine met his eyes once again and smiled. "This Devil's Stone you're looking for . . . I suppose you know there's a chance you might not find it, right? And then you'd be stuck here forever."

"Yes."

"Well, if that happened, would it really be so awful?"

Greg blinked, surprised by the question. His gut response was to say, *Of course it would*. But now, he realized, that wasn't quite right.

"What I'm trying to say," Catherine went on, "is that I don't want you to go."

"You don't?" Greg asked.

"No," Catherine said. "I admit there have been times when I have been wary of you. Even frightened, perhaps. And then, when I learned you were from the future, I didn't really know what to make of that. But now, after all we've been through together, things have changed. And I've come to realize that I . . . Well, when I saw that building explode and I thought you were in it, I couldn't bear the thought of you being dead. And now that I have you back, I don't want to lose you again."

Greg turned to Catherine, astonished. Unable to believe that someone was saying such things to him. Especially someone as wonderful as Catherine. Suddenly, he knew that he felt the same way about her.

And yet, it still didn't change the fact that he desperately wanted to go home.

Catherine turned away, mistaking his hesitance for disinterest. "I see," she said sadly. "You don't feel the same way."

"That's not true!" Greg said. "Not at all! Catherine, you're the most amazing girl I've ever met in my life. I just can't believe that I had to come all the way back to 1615 to do it."

Catherine brightened, her eyes alive with excitement. "So . . . If you had to stay here, you wouldn't mind being with me?"

"No," Greg said. Which was the truth. *If* he had to stay here. And for a moment, he actually found himself conflicted. Could he actually be happy in 1615 with all the lice and disease and poor sanitation? Could he be happy without books and movies and ice cream and the millions of other things he missed from the future? All he'd wanted to do ever since he got here was get home, and now even doing that wasn't going to be easy.

"D'Artagnan?" someone asked in surprise.

Greg looked up. He and Catherine had reached the small plaza before the front entrance of the Louvre. It was now surrounded by members of the king's guard—far more than had been posted before Greg had left. Obviously, security had been beefed up during the siege. It was one of the guards who had called his name. Greg recognized him from his time living at the palace. Several others were staring at him in disbelief.

"Yes," Greg replied. "I have returned."

To his surprise, all the guards pulled out their swords. Within seconds, he and Catherine were surrounded, eight blades aimed at their chests.

"By decree of the king, you are hereby under arrest," a guard informed them.

"For what?" Greg gasped.

"Treason," the guard replied.

TEN

After disarming them, the guards marched Greg and Catherine through the palace to the throne room. King Louis XIII was waiting for them.

As Louis was only Greg's age—and small at that—he still looked like a mere boy playing king on the throne. But his demeanor toward Greg had changed radically, and Greg saw it immediately. Before, Louis had considered Greg a friend and had always been eager to see him. Now, based on his stern expression and narrowed eyes, he regarded Greg with suspicion and anger.

Greg and Catherine were brought before the throne and forced to their knees. The guards stood behind them, keeping their swords drawn.

"How dare you show your face here?" Louis said to Greg.

"Louis, I don't know what you think I've done," Greg pleaded, "but you're making a terrible mistake. I've been nothing but loyal to you—"

"Loyal?" the king snapped. "You and all the other Musketeers played me for a fool. You tricked me into sending my army out of the city so Condé could take Paris."

"No! We did no such thing," Greg protested. "Milady de Winter sent you those messages, not us!"

"I told you he'd say that, didn't I?" The voice was beautiful, but it sent a chill through Greg's bones. Milady de Winter emerged from the shadows in the corner of the room. She wore a regal white dress and looked more stunning than ever. Louis's gaze was riveted to her. Milady, however, kept her eyes locked on Greg and Catherine. Greg thought she looked like a cat staring at two mice it was about to play with.

"Yes," Louis said obediently. "You did." As Milady arrived at his throne, he took her hand.

Oh no, Greg thought. It was evident that Louis had fallen for Milady, just as Aramis and Athos had.

"Such a foolish and desperate argument," Milady said. "Anyone could see those messages were in Aramis's writing, not mine."

"Only the first one was," Greg countered. "She faked his writing in the others. There really was a Spanish army. But we defeated it—and then Milady betrayed us."

"You betrayed *me*," Milady spat. "You tried to kill me and left me for dead." She turned back to Louis and stared lovingly into his eyes. "It was only through a miracle that I was able to return to your side."

"Don't listen to her!" Greg said. "*She's* the double-crosser here! She's aligned with Condé! She engineered this entire siege, and she's plotting to kill you—"

"Silence!" Louis roared. "Milady is the one who has been loyal here. The moment she learned of your plot, she raced back to the city to inform me of it. You're the one who plots to kill me."

"If I was plotting to kill you, why would I just walk right up to the palace?" Greg asked.

"Because you didn't count on Milady beating you back here," Louis replied. "You expected to simply walk in here, pretending to be my friend, and then slit my throat."

"Louis, please," Greg pleaded. "I *am* your friend. I'm telling the truth. If you want proof, question Catherine and me separately. We'll tell you the exact same thing."

"All that will prove is that you've rehearsed your story well," Milady said, then turned to Louis. "Why do you even let him continue spewing these lies? Let's just find out what we need to from him."

Louis snapped his fingers, and his guards all pointed their swords at Greg again. "Where are the other Musketeers?" the king demanded.

"They are working to protect this city from Condé," Greg replied. "They are working to protect your throne, unaware that Milady has poisoned your mind against them—"

"Enough lies!" Louis yelled. "Tell me where they are!"

"I don't know where they are," Greg said. "We had to split up."

Milady whispered something in Louis's ear. The king nodded agreement, then looked back at Greg. "It appears you need some extra motivation to tell the truth." He signaled to some guards across the room.

They opened the door, revealing Greg's parents.

They were flanked by more guards, who marched them into the throne room. Both of them were at once thrilled to see Greg and bewildered by what was happening.

"Mom! Dad!" Greg called. "Are you all right?"

"We are now," his father replied.

"Thank goodness you're alive," his mother said. "We've been so worried about you." She started toward Greg, but the guards blocked her path and aimed their swords at her.

"Now then, D'Artagnan," Milady said. "Tell us where the other Musketeers are—or your parents will suffer." As she spoke, Greg caught sight of something silver glistening just beneath the neckline of her dress: the chain that half

the Devil's Stone hung from. She was wearing it. Milady seemed aware that he'd noticed and smiled cruelly.

Greg seethed with anger, but he willed himself to stay calm. Athos had taught him that if he ever found himself in a tight spot, he needed to keep focused. He might not be as good a fighter as Athos, but Athos had trained him well, and he was certainly better than any guard in this room. Greg met Milady's eyes. "Okay," he said. "The other Musketeers are in Paris."

"We know that much." Milady took a few steps forward and looked down her nose at Greg. "The question is, *where* in Paris?"

"Look behind me," Greg replied.

Milady looked up reflexively. So did Louis. And, as Greg had predicted, so did the guards surrounding him.

In that second, Greg sprang to his feet and took out the closest guard, kicking his legs out from under him and snatching the sword from his hand as he fell. The other guards wheeled back toward him, but before they could attack, Greg had already lunged for Milady. He caught her arm, spun her so that he stood behind her, and placed the sharp steel of his blade against her neck. "Back down!" he ordered the guards.

They all froze, unsure what to do.

"D'Artagnan!" Louis cried. "Don't hurt her!"

"Let my parents and Catherine go," Greg countered. "Or I'll cut her throat."

"Don't give in to him," Milady told the king. "He's bluffing."

"I'm not," Greg said. "If I had anyone else in this position, I would be. But not with you, Milady." With that, he pressed his blade harder against her neck.

Milady's cool facade faded. When she spoke again, there was fear in her voice. "Louis, I was wrong. Do what he says."

Louis turned to his guards. "You heard her! Back away from the prisoners!"

The guards obeyed, lowering their swords.

"Drop your weapons," Greg told them.

A dozen swords clattered to the floor.

Catherine leaped to her feet, grabbing the weapons around her and moving toward the door. Greg's parents took her cue and did the same.

"And now," Greg whispered in Milady's ear, "I'd like the amulet you're wearing. It belongs to my family."

"You'll have to take it yourself, if you don't mind," Milady said coolly. "I can't remove it with this sword to my throat."

With his free hand, Greg unlatched the chain from Milady's neck and lifted it up. The moment the Devil's Stone came into view, everyone in the room gasped, aware there was something unearthly about it.

"My amulet!" Greg's mother cried. "How did she get it?"

"I'll explain later," Greg said. In his hand, he could feel the stone pulsating with power. "You have something else of mine," he told Milady. "The little magic box you find so fascinating."

"It's right here." Milady reached into the folds of her dress and fumbled around inside. "You'll forgive me if this takes a moment. Oops. . . ." Something tumbled from her dress and shattered on the floor at her feet.

Greg reflexively glanced down. The broken object was a glass perfume vial, not his phone. Milady had tricked him into losing focus. Before he could recover, she jammed an elbow into his stomach, knocking the wind out of him, then spun free of his grasp. At the same time, she swept his legs out from under him, then yanked the amulet from his grasp as he crashed to the floor.

Greg couldn't believe how quickly it happened. In all the time he'd known Milady, he'd never had any idea she could fight. As usual, he'd underestimated her.

He sprang back to his feet to find she was already halfway to the door, the Devil's Stone in her hand. His father and Catherine tried to block her path, but she dodged both like a cat. Greg took off after her.

"Stop him!" Louis yelled to his guards.

The men came at Greg, but Catherine and his parents had taken their weapons. Greg slashed his sword at them, and they shrank back in fear.

"Come on!" Greg told Mom, Dad, and Catherine. "We can't let Milady get away!"

They followed him out of the throne room, and the

guards pursued them. Greg caught a glimpse of Milady ducking around a corner ahead and went after her. They raced through the palace—through the grand ballroom, a waiting room, and the main kitchen. Milady upended a huge pot off the central stove, sending a wave of boiling water surging toward Greg. He sprang on a crate of cabbage to avoid it, then grabbed onto the huge rack of pots and pans that hung from the ceiling and swung across the water. By the time he was on his feet again, Milady was disappearing out the far door.

Greg raced into the next room—a preparation chamber for feasts—only to find that Milady had vanished. He pushed on into the next hallway. Milady wasn't here, either. Instead, a phalanx of the king's guard was charging up the grand staircase.

"There he is!" the leader shouted.

Greg had no choice but to retreat back into the preparation chamber, where he almost bowled Catherine over as she emerged from the kitchen with his parents. "Milady's gone," he said. "And the king's guard has us surrounded."

"Not necessarily," Catherine told him. She yanked down on one of the oil lamps that jutted from the wall. There was a click, and a set of shelves swung out from the wall like a door, revealing a secret passage.

Greg and his parents followed Catherine inside and pulled the door shut behind them. They could hear both factions of the king's guard arrive on the other side a moment later and express concern as to which way their quarry had gone.

The secret passage was extremely narrow, barely a foot across. Greg and his parents followed Catherine through it quickly.

"Milady must have come this way, too," Greg surmised. "How did you know about it?"

"I've seen her use it before," Catherine confided. "There are dozens throughout the palace. Louis's father had them all put in while the Louvre was being remodeled. He wanted to be able to escape if the palace were ever overrun. Louis himself might not even know about all of them—although Milady certainly does. She used them all the time."

"Greg, who is this girl?" his mother asked.

"This is Catherine," Greg said. "We can trust her. She knows the truth about where we're from. I promise, I'll explain more later. But right now, we need to find Milady to get your amulet and my phone back."

They came to a fork in the passage. A hallway went to the left, while a narrow set of stairs went up to the right.

"Which way?" Greg asked Catherine.

Catherine started up the stairs. "Milady has a secret little room up here. She doesn't know I know about it."

The stairs corkscrewed upward in a tight spiral. As they climbed, Greg realized he hadn't even had a chance to say a proper hello to his parents after not seeing them for weeks. "I'm sorry," he told them. "I didn't think our reunion was going to be like this. Have you been all right while I've been gone?"

"For the most part, yes," his father replied. "Everything has been fine. Your mother's health has actually improved greatly while you've been away. She seems to have gotten over her trauma after being imprisoned in La Mort."

"Really?" Greg asked. "That's great, Mom!"

"But then, two days ago, that horrid Milady returned and everything changed," Mom continued. "The next thing your father and I knew, we were prisoners. They locked us in our room here, and we weren't allowed out until the guards came for us just now."

"How were your travels?" Dad asked.

"Very interesting," Greg said. "I'll tell you all about it when we have more time."

They reached the top of the stairs. They had come up so many flights, Greg figured they had to be almost at the top of the palace. The ceiling here sloped sharply, matching the steep pitch of the roof. There was a small landing facing a wooden door.

The door was locked, but the wood was flimsy. Greg threw his shoulder into it, and it tore apart. He stumbled into what was obviously Milady's secret room.

It had probably been designed as an attic space, but Milady had commandeered it for her own purposes. It was surprisingly large, with a high ceiling formed by the roof of the Louvre directly above. A long table was stacked high with books, scrolls, and other documents that Milady had most likely stolen. There were two other doors, allowing her access to other hidden passages. Daylight streamed through two vents in the ceiling, making it better lit than most of the rooms in the palace.

Milady herself stood in the center of the room. Rather than appear surprised by Greg's intrusion, she seemed pleased by it. "Welcome," she said with a smile. "I'm so pleased you could make it."

It's a trap, Greg thought, and he turned to warn the others. But he was too late. There were four men behind them, blocking the way out. Greg recognized all of them. He'd last seen them in the woods near the Pont du Gard. Three were members of Condé's army. And the fourth—the handsome man with the devilish grin—was the Prince of Condé himself.

ELEVEN

"Drop your weapons," Condé ordered.

Greg had no choice. He let his sword fall. Catherine and his parents dropped the weapons they'd been carrying as well.

"I am impressed. You are a very difficult person to kill," Condé told Greg. "I have no idea how you escaped from Les Baux. Apparently, if I want you dead, I'll have to kill you myself." He took a step toward Greg. The blade of his sword flashed in the light.

"Not yet," Milady said sharply.

Condé stopped in his tracks like a well-trained dog. "Why not?"

"He still has information that is of value to us," Milady replied.

"I already told you, I don't know where the other Musketeers are," Greg said.

"I very much doubt that's true." Milady sighed. "However, there is *other* information I need from you. Something I couldn't bring up in front of the king." She held up the amulet, letting the piece of the Devil's Stone dangle before Greg's eyes. "Where is the other half of this?"

"I don't know," Greg said.

Milady came closer, studying him carefully. "Now *that* I believe. But you have some idea as to where it might be, yes? You and Aramis have been working hard on this, because Dinicoeur *does* know where the other half is, correct?"

"Yes," Greg said. Denying it seemed pointless. Milady probably already knew the truth.

Milady smiled. "The real question is, exactly what can this stone do when both halves are brought together?"

"I don't know," Greg said again.

"Back to lying now, are you?" Milady asked. "That is very disappointing, Gregory."

Greg flinched in surprise. It was the first time he'd ever heard Milady say his real name.

She smiled in response. "Oh, yes. I know much more about you than I've let on." She turned to Condé. "Keep an eye on the parents and Catherine. I need to talk to Gregory here in private."

"But . . . ," Condé began, looking concerned.

"Don't worry," Milady said. She picked up Greg's sword off the floor and jabbed it into Greg's back. "He won't cause me any trouble."

With that, she forced Greg through one of the other doors and into a much smaller room, barely bigger than a closet. When Milady spun Greg around to face her, there were only a few inches between them. Although Milady kept the point of her sword tucked just below Greg's chin, there was no longer loathing in her eyes. Instead, she actually looked friendly.

"I know you think you're doing the chivalrous thing by refusing to tell me what I want to know," she said. "But you're fighting a losing battle. There are more of Condé's men inside the city than just those in the other room. Tonight, they will take the city gates by surprise from the inside. Then they'll allow the army through, and Paris will fall. Meanwhile, Condé will murder Louis in his sleep. And just like that, Paris will have a new king. There is nothing you or your Musketeers can do about it."

Greg tried to remain tough before Milady. He didn't want to give her the pleasure of seeing him crack. But he couldn't do it. He knew she wasn't bluffing about her plans—and the truth was, he *didn't* know how to prevent it from happening. Tonight, despite everything he'd done, despite everything he'd been through, world history was going to change.

However, Milady didn't seem pleased by the effect this information had on Greg. Instead, she seemed concerned. "Now, now," she said, placing a comforting hand on his arm. "There's no need to be so unhappy. In fact, there's a very good opportunity here for you. The next king of France doesn't necessarily have to be Condé."

Greg's eyes went wide. He stared at Milady in disbelief. *No*, he thought. *She couldn't possibly be that duplicitous.*

"Yes," Milady said, as though she'd read his thoughts. "I mean you."

"I thought you loved Condé," Greg said. "I thought you were going to be his queen."

"In the history of royalty, love has never been a prerequisite for being a queen," Milady countered. "Royal marriages have always been about one thing: power. Now, Condé has the means to overthrow the throne—although frankly, he never would have been able to pull it off without me. But once that's done, he brings very little to the equation. He's nice to look at, but he's not very bright. You, on the other hand, are very clever. Far smarter than just about anyone else I've met. But then, I suspect that's because you're from the future, correct?"

Greg did his best to hide his surprise that Milady knew this. "That's not true," Greg said weakly.

"Oh come now," Milady said. "There's no use denying

it. I'm quite intelligent myself. Certainly smart enough to know that nothing like this could have been built in this day and age." With that, she held up Greg's phone.

Greg stared at it. He was relieved to see it was still intact and could still get him home again. But Milady was currently holding all the cards. Right now, there didn't seem to be anything he could do except play along with her.

"You're right," he said. "I'm from the future."

Milady grinned, pleased with herself. "How far in the future?"

"About four hundred years."

For once, Milady looked surprised. "So then, Dinicoeur isn't Richelieu's twin at all? He's a descendant of his from the future?"

Greg didn't answer right away, and Milady rightfully understood that his hesitation was an answer in itself. She stepped back, and Greg could see that her mind was racing. A look of fascination overcame her as she put everything together. "No," she said. "He's not a descendant. He's Richelieu himself! My goodness, this stone doesn't merely make time travel possible. It can also make one immortal?"

"Yes," Greg admitted. "Though I think Dinicoeur has learned that's not as great as it sounds."

"Then we can learn from his mistakes," Milady said. "What else can the stone do?"

"That's it," Greg lied. "Isn't that enough for you?"

Milady didn't catch his lie; she was too distracted with visions of glory.

"Yes," she said. "That could be very handy indeed. So I want you to think very carefully about your choices, Gregory. If you try to stand in my way, things won't work out well for you—and your family and your girlfriend out there will be lucky to survive the next five minutes. But if you work with me and help get the other half of this stone, the world will be ours for the taking. Just imagine combining the power of the throne with the power of the stone. We could create an empire bigger than that of Alexander the Great, Julius Caesar, or Genghis Khan . . . and we could rule it for eternity. Now which sounds better to you?"

Despite his best instincts, Greg found himself disturbingly tempted by Milady's offer. It certainly made a twisted sort of sense. Taking the moral high ground sounded great in theory, but what good would it do if it only got him and the people he cared about killed? Why not team up with Milady instead and become rich, powerful, and immortal? He could help everyone then. As Greg stared into Milady's gorgeous blue eyes, he found himself thinking that it wouldn't be so bad to have her as his queen as well. True, she had betrayed him before, but she was so beautiful. . . .

No, he thought. *What am I thinking?* And then, he found himself wondering if it was even *him* thinking at all. There was something eerily hypnotic about Milady's stare. And now that Greg thought about it, he could almost feel her mind working on his, Milady trying to worm her way into his consciousness. His eyes flicked to the Devil's Stone. It seemed to be pulsing in her hand somehow. If he concentrated, he could feel the energy from it.

Could the Devil's Stone let you control people's minds? Greg knew this piece had powers by itself. Or maybe it could just enhance a person's normal abilities. After all, his mother had worn it plenty of times—but then, she'd never known that the stone had any powers and thus would never have tried to use them. Milady, on the other hand, was determined to harness the stone's strength. Without it, she was already the most manipulative person Greg had ever met. With it, she seemed almost impossible to refuse. That would explain how quickly she'd bent King Louis to her will, how smitten he'd become with her. . . .

And she planned to betray him.

The same went for Condé. He, too, was willing to do anything for her, and now Milady was confiding to Greg that she would happily toss him aside as well.

Which meant that if Greg accepted Milady's offer, she'd most likely betray him, too. Milady didn't care about him. She didn't care about anyone except herself. All she wanted from Greg was his help finding the other half of the Devil's Stone. Once he did that, he'd no longer be of any use to her. In fact, the only reason he was still alive was because Milady thought he knew far more than he actually did about where the other half was.

Realizing this, Greg suddenly felt immune to Milady's power. He would use this situation to at least save Catherine and his parents. And he'd try to leverage his new "alliance" to get more information about Condé's plans. He looked back into Milady's eyes. He no longer saw her as beautiful and enticing, but as the cruel and calculating person he knew she was.

He didn't let Milady know this, however. Instead, he acted as though he'd been completely entranced by her. He tried to mimic the smitten expression he'd seen on King Louis. "You're right," he said. "Ruling an empire does sound better. Especially with you by my side."

Milady smiled coyly and batted her eyes. "I know we've had our differences in the past," she said. "But I've always thought you were very handsome."

"Just to be clear, though," Greg said. "If we do this, my parents and Catherine don't get hurt. You'll let them go right now?"

Milady finally lowered her sword from Greg's neck. "Right now," she said reassuringly.

"And you'll tell the king that they are no threat to him and neither am I?"

"Of course." Milady leaned so close to Greg, he could feel her breath on him. "And then, you and I will go find the other half of this stone."

Greg felt himself being enticed again. *Don't trust her,* he had to remind himself. *Just play along until you figure out what to do.* "Yes," he said. "I'll do whatever you want me to do."

Milady pulled away from him, smiling. "You've made a very good decision," she said.

There suddenly came the sounds of a scuffle on the other side of the door, followed by several startled cries. Milady quickly threw open the door—only to find Michel Dinicoeur waiting on the other side.

TWELVE

CONDÉ AND HIS MEN WERE SPRAWLED ON THE ATTIC FLOOR behind Dinicoeur, out cold. They'd been taken by surprise so quickly they hadn't even put up a fight. Greg's parents and Catherine were still conscious, cowering in a corner. Dominic Richelieu held them at sword point. Either he was unaware that Dinicoeur had made a last-ditch attempt to kill Stefan, or he'd gotten over it.

For a moment, Greg thought that Dinicoeur and Milady might have teamed up against him, but then Milady screamed in horror, and Greg realized she wasn't faking.

Dinicoeur had caught her by surprise as well. She hadn't expected that he'd find her here—and she obviously hadn't seen what had happened to him since the Pont du Gard.

She tried to raise her sword against him, but he shoved her backward into Greg, and both of them fell to the floor. The phone clattered to the ground. The amulet flew from Milady's hand and Dinicoeur caught it in midair. "You really think I didn't know about your little hideout here?" he snarled at Milady, dangling the amulet tauntingly. "This is the price you pay for foolishness." With that, he pulled another grenade from the satchel that hung around his neck, touched the wick to one of the lamps in the room, and tossed it at Greg before fleeing with Richelieu.

The grenade bounded across the floor and plunked into Greg's lap. Greg glanced at the wick. It was almost burnt out already. There might have been time for him to run, but his parents and Catherine were too far from the door. They'd be blown to bits.

There were only a few seconds to act. Greg snatched the grenade, leaped onto the table in the center of the room, then slam-dunked the bomb through one of the ceiling vents. It tumbled down the edge of the roof and exploded outside. The room shook violently from the blast, and centuries' worth of dust dislodged from the ceiling, but no one was hurt.

Catherine quickly grabbed Condé's sword and started toward one of the doors. "They went this way!" she told

Greg. "We can still catch up to them."

"Let me go after them," Greg told her, grabbing his phone and stuffing it into the folds of his clothes. "Tie up Milady and Condé and their men and then get my parents to Notre Dame. I'll meet up with all of you there." Before Catherine or his parents could protest, he raced out of the room.

It felt wonderful to have his phone back, but it wouldn't do him any good if Dinicoeur had the Devil's Stone. Even though he was outnumbered and worn out, he had no choice but to go after them.

The door his enemies had fled through led to another narrow staircase, which in turn took Greg upward to a trapdoor in the ceiling. He scrambled through it and suddenly found himself on the roof of the palace. The Louvre varied greatly in height from place to place, so the roof had many levels, and Greg now found himself at its highest point. In fact, save for the bell towers of Notre Dame, he was at the highest point in all of Paris, a small flat area atop a dramatic peak of the roof, ten stories above the main entrance to the castle. Nearby, the roof slanted downward steeply toward a much larger stretch that covered the northern wing of the Louvre. From where he stood, Greg could see down into the courtyard, which served as a training ground for the military. Much of the palace below was lined by several stories of scaffolding, as the building was still under construction. Lots of workmen and a dozen members of the king's guard were staring up toward him. The explosion of the grenade had probably drawn their attention, but now he, Dinicoeur, and Richelieu had it.

Dinicoeur and Richelieu had disappeared over the edge of the roof. Greg found them scurrying down a ladder built into the steep incline toward the northern wing. Rather than take the time to climb down the ladder, he simply leaped onto the steep slope and slid down it. He rocketed over the smooth slate tiles and hit the lower roof just behind his enemies.

Greg was still eight stories above the ground. A narrow, level walkway ran straight down the middle of the roof, but from there, each side slanted precariously toward a stone railing studded with massive statues of gods and cherubs.

"Hold him off!" Dinicoeur ordered, and Richelieu withdrew his sword, blocking the narrow walkway, while his older self scurried off with the amulet.

Greg held up his sword as well and fended off the attack. "How can you still trust him?" he asked Richelieu. "He tried to kill your son!"

"And he stopped when I told him not to," Richelieu replied. "He was trying to do what was best for us. He and I are the same, after all."

"No," Greg said. "You're not the same. He's too obsessed with revenge to think about what's best for you anymore."

"That's not true!" Richelieu shouted, and charged Greg again.

"Really?" Greg asked, parrying. "He left a grenade in Teresa's house after you two fled. Even after you told him not to, he still tried to kill your son."

Richelieu paused, and in that moment Greg saw that he'd guessed right: Although Richelieu and Dinicoeur had the same body, they were not exactly the same man anymore. Richelieu's mind hadn't been warped by centuries of anger and plotting revenge. Not yet. He wasn't a good man, but at least he seemed capable of reason. And yet he still couldn't bring himself to believe that Greg's words were true. "No," he said.

"You heard the explosion, didn't you?" Greg asked.

"That was one of Condé's cannons firing at the city."

Greg shook his head. "No, it wasn't," he said simply.

"He would never betray me like that!" Richelieu's eyes filled with anger. Perhaps it was at Dinicoeur, but he directed it toward Greg, attacking again.

Behind Richelieu, Greg could see Dinicoeur getting away. He was carefully picking his way down the roof to a place where the scaffolding was highest. His good hand clutched the amulet, the Devil's Stone gleaming darkly in the light of the setting sun. If Dinicoeur got away with it now, Greg doubted he'd ever get it back.

"He *did* betray you," Greg told Richelieu. "And you know it. He's insane. He's so determined to have his revenge on me and the Musketeers that he's willing to kill his own son. *Your* son."

"No!" Richelieu yelled again. He charged, full of fury, slashing his sword.

Greg sidestepped him on the narrow walkway, letting Richelieu's momentum carry him past, then raced after Dinicoeur. Richelieu recovered and took up the chase.

Suddenly, an arrow whistled past Greg's ear.

Down in the courtyard, the king's guard had recognized him. Now they were opening fire as well—as though *he* were the enemy here.

Great, Greg thought. *As if I didn't have enough going on right now.*

He reached the point where Dinicoeur had gone down the roof. There was no time for caution; Greg simply ran down the slant. Another arrow came flying toward him. He dodged it, but stumbled and picked up too much momentum on the slope. He flew down the incline and slammed into the railing so hard that he pitched over it. His legs flipped over his head and for one dizzying moment, he fell.

And then he slammed into the scaffolding. He landed flat on his back on the wooden planks. He'd only dropped ten feet, but it was enough to knock the wind out of him. He sat up, his ears ringing, and saw Dinicoeur racing down the scaffold not far ahead. Greg might have taken a bad fall—but he'd gained a lot of ground.

He'd also lost his sword, however. He spotted it teetering

on the edge of a plank, but as he lunged for it, it fell and tumbled into the courtyard.

It landed at the feet of the soldiers, who loaded a new round of arrows into their bows.

Greg looked around desperately for a new plan. There was a pallet full of masonry—huge pieces of limestone for the facade of the palace—dangling from a winch nearby. A chunk of wood had been wedged into the pulley to keep it from moving. Greg snatched up a piece of lumber the size of a baseball bat and smacked the chunk as hard as he could. It popped loose, releasing the pallet, which plummeted downward.

The soldiers scattered as it crashed into the ground where they'd just been standing. A thick cloud of limestone dust billowed into the air, creating a smoke screen for Greg to escape. He charged after Dinicoeur.

The scaffolding shook as Richelieu dropped onto it behind Greg.

Dinicoeur tried to flee into the palace. He heaved a piece of masonry through a window and started to climb inside, but Greg caught up to him before he could. Greg lowered his shoulder and slammed into Dinicoeur with all his might, and the two of them cartwheeled along the scaffold. The amulet tumbled free and bounded over the edge.

Greg dove and, at the last moment, caught the final link of the silver chain.

Then he scrambled away just as Dinicoeur lunged for

him. He almost made it, but Dinicoeur snagged his heel and latched on like a pit bull. "Give me the stone!" he roared.

Greg looked into the disgusting mask of burnt flesh. At this range, he could smell Dinicoeur as well. The man had a nauseating stench, like meat that had gone bad.

Behind him on the scaffolding, Richelieu was bearing down, his sword aimed right for Greg's chest.

Greg spotted a rope that dangled down the scaffolding, attached to a winch high above. He grabbed onto it and, with his free leg, booted Dinicoeur in the mouth. Dinicoeur howled in pain, releasing his grip on Greg's leg.

Greg leaped off the scaffold just as Richelieu slashed at him. He felt the wind as the sword sliced the air beside him. He swung out on the rope, away from the scaffold and his enemies—and straight toward a huge window. There was no way Greg could alter his course. All he could do was brace for impact. He smashed through the glass, sailed into the palace, and rolled across the floor.

A chorus of screams greeted his arrival.

Greg looked up to find he'd landed in the laundry room, with a dozen laundresses staring at him.

"Sorry for the intrusion," Greg told them, and ran for the door.

Out the window behind him, he could hear Dinicoeur far away on the scaffolding, bellowing with rage. "That stone won't be yours for long!" he roared. "I'll find you again long before you ever find the other half!"

Greg didn't even look back. He just ran on through the palace, determined to quickly get as far away as he could.

He hung the amulet around his neck as he ran, but still kept his hand clenched around the stone. He couldn't believe he actually had it again—as well as his phone—but he was all too aware how quickly this prize had slipped through his fingers before. He wasn't familiar with all the secret passages like Catherine, but he did know some less traveled ways through the palace after the months he'd lived there. He moved quickly through rarely used rooms and down forgotten staircases, finally reaching an unguarded door.

He stepped out into the streets of Paris. To the west, he could see the summer sun sinking behind the city wall. That made it around nine o'clock at night. Greg felt as though he'd been moving constantly for almost eighteen hours. He'd never been so exhausted in his life. And yet there was still much more he had to do. Although every part of his body ached with fatigue, he quickly started through the alleys toward Notre Dame.

He hadn't gotten more than a few steps when several men suddenly stepped from the shadows, surrounding him. "D'Artagnan! Stop!" one ordered.

Greg whirled around. The men were coming at him from all sides. He could see their uniforms now—the king's guard. There were too many of them to outrun, and even if he had been talented enough to fight them all, he had no weapon. He slipped the amulet into his shirt and raised his hands in defeat.

The guard directly ahead of him broke into laughter. Then he stepped into the light of the setting sun, revealing his face.

Athos.

THIRTEEN

"You don't have to worry," Athos told Greg. He
pointed to a young man who wore the uniform of a captain.
"This is Henri, another good friend from my days in the
guard. You can trust him."

Henri bowed formally. "I understand your concern
around us, however. Some of my fellow guardsmen do not
realize that the king has been"—Henri paused to choose
his words carefully—"*compromised* lately."

"About a dozen of them just tried to kill me," Greg said.

"Then we'd best get as far away from the palace as

possible," Henri said. "They are most likely still looking for you. While my own men are loyal to me, the others will remain loyal to the king." With that, he led the way into the alleys of Paris.

"I had my own encounter with the king's guard," Athos explained as they hurried through the town. "When I went to the Bastille, they arrested me. Luckily, Henri here was the commander. When he found out what had happened, he had me released."

"Why didn't you just tell your men that the king was wrong about us when he issued the order?" Greg asked Henri.

"I had no idea you were alive!" Henri replied. "Or at the very least, I thought you were on the other side of France. There didn't seem to be much point in telling my men to disobey a direct order from the king in those circumstances. When my men told me they had taken a Musketeer prisoner, I thought they were crazy."

"The moment Henri had me released, we came to find you," Athos said. "I knew that if the king's guard was aligned against us, you'd walked right into the lion's den. Though it looks like you got out okay."

"It wasn't easy," Greg said. "The king's guard is the least of our problems. Milady is back. She's the one who turned the king against us. I'm not sure, but she might have hypnotized him somehow. With this." He held up the amulet.

"The stone!" Athos crowed. "You got it back!"

"That wasn't so easy, either," Greg told him.

"So, if she doesn't have the stone, does that mean she doesn't have power over the king anymore?" Athos asked.

"Maybe, maybe not," Greg admitted. "As you know, Milady can be awfully persuasive on her own. . . ." He caught himself before he went any further, thinking he might have upset Athos.

Athos just laughed, however, as if everything Milady had done to him was forgotten. "Yes. That girl's mind is as dangerous as any sword."

"The good news is, Milady has been captured. Catherine and my parents have her tied up in a secret room at the top of the palace." Greg decided not to share the part about the deal Milady had offered him. It would only complicate things. "We also captured Condé and three of his men."

Athos and Henri reacted with astonishment. "Inside the palace?" Henri asked.

"They snuck into the city through one of the secret passages," Greg explained.

"Well, no more of Condé's men will be able to do that," Henri replied. "I have sent my men to seal all the passages off."

Greg shook his head. "It's too late. Condé already has men in the city. They're going to attack the city gates from the inside tonight. Once they take them, they'll open them up for the army to come through."

Athos and Henri exchanged a worried look. "Do you have

any idea which gates they plan to attack?" Athos asked.

Greg shook his head. "No. Sorry."

"There's nothing to be sorry about. The information you did get may save this city." Henri turned to his men. "We need to get word to each of the city gates to be prepared for an attack from the inside this very night." He pointed to each of his men in turn, naming a gate. They saluted and ran off without a moment's hesitation. However, there were only thirteen guardsmen—and fourteen gates. "I shall return to the Bastille myself," Henri told Athos. "I could use a warrior such as you, should this battle happen."

"My leg isn't completely healed, but I'll do what I can," Athos said. "But first, I need to make sure Greg gets to safety."

"Wait!" Greg said before Henri could go. "What about Condé and Milady? We can't leave them tied up in the attic forever."

"Why not?" Henri asked with a smirk. "They can starve to death for all I care."

"I think there's a better chance of them escaping long before that happens," Greg warned. "All it takes is for one of them to get out of their bonds. Then they free the others, and suddenly we have assassins loose in the palace again, hunting the king."

"Good point," Athos said. "If anyone could be expected to worm out of a situation like this, it's Milady. How long ago did you leave her?"

"Fifteen minutes," Greg said. "Maybe a bit more."

"And where is this attic?" Henri asked.

"It's a secret room up in one of the highest points in the palace," Greg told them. "To be honest, I don't know if I could find my way there again. But Catherine could tell you how to get there."

"And where is Catherine?" Athos asked.

"Hopefully, she's back at Notre Dame by now," Greg said. "Along with my parents."

Henri turned to Athos. "Take D'Artagnan to Notre Dame and find out where Condé is. I'll send a team of men back there to escort you to the palace."

"I can handle this myself," Athos said. "You need every man you have guarding the gates."

"Don't be a fool, Athos," Henri said. "Never reject help when it's offered to you. Besides, you know your chess, right? The best way to defeat an army is to take its king. Good luck to you this night!" With that, he raced off toward the Bastille.

By now, Greg and Athos had made good progress across the city. The towers of Notre Dame rose close by. The boys cut across the Bridge of Saint Denis, where the remnants of the cheese shop still smoldered, and then raced across the Île de la Cité.

As they pushed on, Athos began to limp, favoring his good leg. Greg glanced down and noticed a dark stain of blood around his wound.

"Maybe we should slow down," Greg said. "You've been going nonstop today."

"Me?" Athos asked. "You've battled the king's guard, Milady, *and* Condé."

"And Dinicoeur and Richelieu," Greg said.

Athos looked at him, impressed. "When?"

"Shortly before I ran into you." Greg told Athos what had happened in more detail. "I'm assuming the king's guard took both of them into custody, though," he concluded. "After all, they know both were traitors to the country."

"Never assume anything where those two are concerned," Athos warned. "If they got away, they'll either be coming after you or lying in wait wherever the second half of the Devil's Stone is. You'd better be on guard."

Greg nodded. "All right. And you'd better take care of yourself. You don't want that leg getting infected again."

"My leg is fine," Athos said, giving Greg a smile. "I owe you my life. I don't think I ever thanked you properly."

"You've saved mine plenty of times," Greg said.

"Yes, and then I turned my back on you." Athos looked away, ashamed. "I was upset at how Milady had used me for a patsy. My pride was wounded and I turned on you, as though *you* were the one I couldn't trust. That was small and petty of me, and I'm sorry."

"And I'm sorry I didn't tell you the truth about myself earlier," Greg said.

"I understand why you didn't. You're from the future.

That makes you awfully . . . peculiar." Athos grinned, letting Greg know he was teasing. "But you're still one of the best friends I've ever had. I'll miss you when you have to go home."

"I'll miss you, too," Greg said, then added, "*if* I ever get the chance to leave."

"Oh, you'll get it," Athos said. "I'm going to make sure of that."

They arrived at the cathedral, and Greg knocked on the huge front doors.

"Who goes there?" a suspicious voice demanded from the other side.

"It's *us*, Porthos," Athos said. "Athos and D'Artagnan."

They heard the bolt on the other side being thrown, and then Porthos peeked out the door. "Hello," he said with a big smile. "Come in."

"I assume from your presence here that you were successful in your mission," Athos said.

"I was," Porthos replied proudly. "Stefan and his mother are hidden away safely where Dinicoeur will never find them." He held the door open wide, allowing the boys inside.

Aramis was right behind Porthos. Inside, the cathedral glowed warmly with candlelight, and everyone Greg cared about was there: his parents, Catherine, and his fellow Musketeers. Greg couldn't imagine a more wonderful sight.

"You're all right!" Catherine ran to him and threw herself into his arms. "We were so worried about you!"

"I was worried about all of you, too," Greg said. "Looks like you made it out of the palace all right."

"You did the hard part, distracting the guards," Catherine said. "We didn't have any trouble."

"And Milady and Condé?" Athos asked.

"We tied them up good and tight," Catherine said. "And Condé's men, too. They're not going anywhere."

Aramis immediately pulled Athos aside to check the bandages on his leg. A little blood had seeped from the wound, but thankfully not too much. "How's your leg holding up?" Aramis asked.

"It still hurts," Athos said. "But not so badly that I can't use it."

Aramis pulled the bandages aside and inspected the wound. "Looks clean," he said. "And the infection certainly seems to be gone. But all your running around is preventing it from healing shut."

"I'll rest once our enemies have been defeated and Paris is saved," Athos told him.

Aramis sighed, but knew there was no point in arguing. "I suppose I'd better prepare you another poultice then." With that, he ducked out the door into the church garden.

As Aramis left, Greg's parents came over to see him. Everything had been so hectic back in the palace, he hadn't had a chance to give either of them a hug yet himself. Now he put his arms around both and held them tight. "I missed you so much," he said.

"Not as much as we missed you," Mom told him.

"I thought I might never see you again," Greg said.

"I can understand why," Dad said. "Catherine told us everything you've been through. You might have died twenty times over."

"We're so sorry you had to go through all that," Mom said. "If only I'd never given my amulet to that horrible Michel Dinicoeur, none of this would have ever happened. I just wish we could go back home again."

"That wish might come true soon." Greg pulled out the amulet and his phone.

His parents gasped in surprise—although Greg thought he caught a glint of disappointment in Catherine's eyes. She recovered and smiled brightly for him. "You got them both? How wonderful."

"Now all we need is the other half of the stone and we can go home," Greg said.

Aramis came back through the door with a handful of fresh herbs for Athos. Greg looked to him expectantly and asked, "Have you learned anything about where the Devil's Stone is hidden?"

"You really ought to be asking your father that," Aramis replied. "He's made some progress while we've been away."

Greg swung back to face his father. "Really? What?"

Greg's father cleared his throat. "Well, before you left, you told me to search through the library here to see if I could find any reference to a White City of Constantine. I've since learned that you actually found that city: Arles. I hadn't figured that out—but I *did* find another reference to the White City in an old scroll. It seems that some Roman legionaires brought a piece of something evil from there to Paris many centuries ago, so far back that the Romans still called Paris Lutetia. They had orders from the emperor to take this thing to the farthest reaches of the Roman Empire."

"That matches the story we heard in Arles!" Greg exclaimed. "The piece of evil they brought has to be the other half of the stone. They were supposed to put it where it would never be found again."

"That's where the stories we've heard differ a bit," Aramis said. He knelt before Athos with a fresh bandage and began to prepare the new poultice.

"Yes," Greg's father said. "I'm guessing those were the Romans' official orders, but it seems that a commander of the legionnaires named Gaius had a different idea. He apparently felt that the stone was too powerful to simply throw away. He hoped that at some point humanity might be better suited for it—that we would have the self-control to use it for good and not evil. Therefore, he wanted to make it possible to retrieve the stone again—but just barely. So he constructed a vault to hold the stone. The vault was made to be impenetrable; only someone who was worthy of the stone would be able to figure out how to get it."

"Obviously, that didn't work out so well," Porthos said, "seeing as the first person to find the stone again was Dinicoeur."

"Did the scroll say where Gaius hid it?" Athos asked.

"No," Greg's father said sadly. "Nothing at all."

"I think it's somewhere under the Louvre," Greg said.

All eyes in the cathedral turned to him.

"You do?" Catherine asked. "Why?"

"Because of something *you* told me back in Arles," Greg replied. "You overheard Dinicoeur tell Richelieu that the second half of the stone was right under the king's nose. That must mean it's in the palace, right?"

Catherine looked at Greg, confused. "I don't understand."

"Greg, 'Under one's nose' is a relatively modern colloquialism," Dad said. "To someone from our time, it means 'close by,' but to someone from this time, it *literally* means the stone is under the king's nose."

"How could the stone *literally* be under the king's nose?" Greg asked.

"Perhaps Louis is wearing the stone on a chain like the one you have," Porthos suggested. "If it was around his neck, it would be under his nose."

"Louis isn't wearing any amulet," Athos chided. "We would have noticed by now."

"Wait!" Aramis cinched the poultice tight on Athos's leg and stood, his eyes alive with excitement. "Maybe Dinicoeur wasn't talking about King Louis at all. What if he meant another king?"

"Another king of France?" Porthos asked. "As far as I remember, there's only one."

"One *living* king," Aramis corrected. "But there are kings in this city who aren't alive."

"You mean dead ones?" Greg asked. "You think the stone's locked away in a tomb somewhere?"

"No," Aramis said. "I mean a king who was *never* alive. As you all may recall, Louis is betrothed to Anne of Austria. The wedding is scheduled for next month."

"Is that still on?" Porthos asked. "Seeing as her father sent an army to overthrow the country?"

"I suspect it is," Athos replied. "Philip is going to want peace with France even more after that. And there's no better way to broker a peace than to marry off your daughter."

"Very well, but what does all this have to do with the king's nose?" Catherine demanded.

"King Louis's mother, Marie de Medici, felt that the marriage should be celebrated with a great gift of art," Aramis explained. "So she commissioned a huge bust of King Louis from Pietro Tacca."

"Pietro Tacca?" Greg's mother asked. "He's the student of Giambologna, right? They did the great sculpture of

Louis's father, King Henry, on the Pont Neuf."

"Yes, although that one isn't finished yet in this time, either," Aramis corrected.

"But Tacca and Giambologna work out of Italy . . . ," Greg's mother began.

"They *did*," Aramis said. "However, for these two works, they set up an artist's studio—an atelier—in Paris. Everyone in the city has been very excited about it. With the unveiling of the bust, Paris will finally become known as a city whose art rivals that of Rome."

"How big is this bust, exactly?" Greg's father asked.

"I'm not sure," Aramis admitted. "No one has seen it yet. But it is supposed to be monumental."

"So then, something located under the bust of King Louis would literally be under the king's nose," Greg said.

"Exactly," Aramis agreed.

"Where's the atelier?" Greg asked.

"Directly across the street from where we're standing," Aramis told him.

"That would explain everything," Greg said excitedly. "The clues we had weren't pointing to two different places in Paris at all."

"What do you mean?" his mother asked.

"We knew two things about the location of the stone," Greg explained. "Dinicoeur said it was right under the king's nose, which I assumed meant the Louvre. And his map indicated a connection with a Crown of Minerva somewhere on the Île de la Cité. But if 'the king's nose' is on the Île de la Cité, then both clues are indicating the same location. The stone must be somewhere on this island."

"Then where is the Crown of Minerva?" Greg's mother asked.

"I don't know yet," Greg admitted. "But I'm sure we'll find it if we start with the bust of King Louis."

"Then what are we waiting for?" Porthos asked. "Let's go find this stone!" He started for the cathedral doors.

"Wait!" Aramis cried. "The atelier is certainly locked up at night. We can't break in. It's against the law."

"We *are* the law," Porthos told him.

"It's morally wrong," Aramis protested.

"The fate of the world is at stake," Porthos countered. "I think we have some moral leeway here." He reached for the doors again, although before he could open them, there was frantic knocking.

Everyone in the cathedral tensed.

"Who goes there?" Porthos demanded in his most commanding voice.

"The emissaries sent by Commander Henri Ducasse," came the reply. "We are here to escort Athos to the palace."

Porthos looked to Athos for confirmation. Athos nodded that it was all right to open the doors.

Four soldiers stood in the plaza before the cathedral. They were all breathing heavily, having run there from the Bastille in full battle gear. The leader, a tall man with a bristling mustache, spoke directly to Athos. "Are you ready to go? Commander Ducasse says our mission is of great urgency."

"I'm ready," Athos said, then looked to Catherine. "Although we need a guide back through the palace to where you left Condé and Milady. I hate to ask a lady to put herself in peril. . . ."

"Then I shall simply volunteer my services," Catherine said. She and Athos headed out of the cathedral. The others rushed after them out into the small plaza before Notre Dame.

Aramis pointed across the plaza to a large building that looked like a warehouse. "That's Pietro Tacca's atelier right there." He started toward it, Porthos and Greg's parents on his heels.

Greg held back, however. He took Catherine by the arm before she could leave. "Be careful," he told her.

"You too," she said with a smile.

Greg stared into her eyes and felt warmth, comfort, and trust in her gaze.

Suddenly, there was an explosion from the direction of the Bastille.

Greg and Catherine turned to see a ball of fire rising

from the city's eastern gate.

"What was that?" Catherine gasped.

"Bad news," Aramis replied. "I think Condé's assault on the gate has already begun."

FOURTEEN

"CHANGE OF PLANS," ATHOS SAID. "I NEED TO HELP PRO-
tect the gate. If it falls, Condé's army will overrun the city."
Without waiting for anyone to respond, he headed off in
the direction of the explosion. He still limped a bit, but if
his leg was causing him any serious pain, he didn't show it.

"Wait!" Porthos called. "What about Condé and
Milady?"

"You go get them!" Athos yelled back. "They've been
tied up. Even you should be able to handle that!" He
flashed a smile, then ducked around the side of the

cathedral and vanished into the night.

"I suppose he's right," Porthos said. "Besides, I won't be any help finding the stone. That will require brains, rather than brawn." He turned to Catherine and the four soldiers Henri had sent. "Let's make haste, shall we?"

The six of them ran off, leaving Greg, his parents, and Aramis in the plaza. Greg noticed that Aramis and his parents all looked very worried. Although he felt concerned himself, it seemed it was up to him to be the confident one. "All right," he said. "Let's find this stone and get back home." He strode purposefully across the plaza to the atelier.

There were two huge doors in front—Greg guessed they needed to be huge to allow the giant sculptures inside to be removed—and they were locked tightly with a hasp and padlock. The windows were shuttered and locked from the inside.

"How are we supposed to get in?" Greg's mother asked.

Aramis pointed up. "There is a large system of louvers in the roof. I have seen it from the bell towers of Notre Dame. I hear that Tacca likes to have natural sunlight in his studio when he works. You're the most nimble of us, D'Artagnan." Aramis glanced at Greg's parents. "I mean Gregory."

"D'Artagnan's fine," Greg said. "It's kind of grown on me." He handed Aramis his sword and studied the facade of the atelier. It was two stories tall and made of rough stone. It wouldn't be the easiest building to scale, but it was still less difficult than plenty of walls he'd faced in the rock gym.

He started up. As his legs and arms were already aching from exertion, he tried to move quickly, so as to put as little strain on them as possible—and yet he'd only gone a few feet before he could feel his strength draining. Still, he pressed on, scrambling from handhold to foothold, until finally, he pulled himself over the lip of the roof and collapsed on the shingles at the top.

"Are you all right?" Aramis called up.

"Yes," Greg replied. "I just need a few moments."

From where he lay, he could see the eastern gate of the city. It was, at most, a half mile away. Flames flickered around it—the result of the explosion, probably—and silhouetted against them, he could see men in the heat of battle. Greg wondered if one of them was Athos; the other Musketeer should have been there by now. Thankfully, the gate still appeared to be standing, although beyond it, Greg could see Condé's army amassed, waiting for the wall to be breached.

Greg was struck by the thought that he was in the wrong place. As a Musketeer, he should have acted like Athos and raced to defend the city. Instead, he was simply trying to find the other half of the Devil's Stone so he could get back home again. Athos had acted selflessly without hesitation, while Greg had not.

No, he thought. *You must find the stone. With the power of the stone, all can be set right.*

Greg realized that the piece of the Devil's Stone, dangling from his neck, had begun to pulse. It was very faint, but it was definitely happening. *Is the stone speaking to me?* he wondered. It seemed impossible, but the stone had done the impossible before.

Greg began to feel energy return to his body. It was almost as though the stone was giving him power. He didn't feel invincible, exactly. It was more that the fatigue in his limbs was ebbing away. He stood up and quickly moved across the roof.

The louvers Aramis had mentioned weren't hard to find: They took up most of the roof. They were a series of giant slats that could be maneuvered to allow the sun in, but keep the rain out. They were designed to be operated by a chain that dangled to the floor; by pulling on it, the sculptor could alter the angle of the louvers above. They were so well constructed that when Greg lifted up on one slat, they all popped open, revealing the workshop floor far below.

He had a way into the atelier; now all he had to do was get two stories down to the floor.

For this, he used the operating chain. He lowered himself through a gap in the louvers, clenched his legs around the chain, and then climbed down it.

The atelier was eerie in the darkness. Everywhere, lurking in the shadows, were the contorted shapes of statues half-completed: headless bodies, limbless torsos, men and women who were part human and part unhewn rock. Greg spotted the half-finished statue of King Henry on horseback. In the future, it would probably look stately and gallant, but for now, it looked like a man and a horse being swallowed by a large piece of stone.

Greg hurried to the plaza window and unlatched it.

The others were waiting. Aramis and Greg's father boosted his mother up, and Greg helped her inside. The others followed quickly, and they locked the shutters again.

There was a fire burning in the fireplace: No one ever let their fire go out in 1615. A torch sat by it. Aramis lit this, then moved about the atelier quickly, lighting the oil lamps. Soon, the atelier was much more inviting, if still a bit shadowy.

It wasn't hard to locate the bust of King Louis. It was the largest sculpture by far, a massive monumental head. The sculptors had taken some liberties with it; rather than merely re-create the awkward teenage face of the current king, they had apparently tried to envision the king in the future. This Louis had aged well. He was handsome and regal, with long, flowing hair and a roguish glint in his eye.

The bust sat prominently in the center of the atelier. The sculptors had obviously been working on it recently. There were ladders and scaffolds around it to allow them access to the upper portions, and the floor surrounding it was thick with marble chips and rock dust. The face appeared finished, however, smooth and clean and free of scaffolding. Greg walked up to it. He could stand directly below Louis's giant nose.

There was nothing there. Only a blank wooden floor.

"Do you think this is the right place?" Greg asked.

Aramis came over and stood with Greg. Then he cocked his head thoughtfully and took a few steps back. Then he returned. Then he took a few steps back again.

"What are you doing?" Greg asked.

"Listen," Aramis said. He walked toward Greg again, placing each foot down firmly and deliberately on the wooden floor. The sound of his footsteps changed subtly as he got closer. There was a bit of an echo to each one.

"It's hollow under the floor!" Greg's father exclaimed.

Greg spotted a rack of large chisels nearby. One was so big—nearly three feet long—he figured it was designed to split chunks of rock in two. He ran over, grabbed it, and brought it back to the spot in front of the bust of Louis. Aramis helped him lift it, and the two of them slammed it into the floor.

Cool, musty air suddenly hissed upward through the cracks between the floorboards, as though it had been trapped below for centuries and was thrilled to escape.

Greg couldn't help but smile. "I think we're on the right track," he said.

He and Aramis wedged the chisel between two floorboards and used it as a crowbar, pressing down on it. Greg's parents rushed to lend a hand. The wood was old and brittle and with a resounding crack, a piece ripped free, leaving a six-inch gap in the floor. Everyone jammed the chisel in again and quickly pried loose another plank and another, so that there was now a big enough hole for a person to fit through.

They all stood around it. Although they couldn't see anything but darkness below, they could sense that they had tapped into something large. To Greg, it felt like standing at the edge of a cave.

Aramis dropped the lit torch through the hole. It fell another ten feet, then landed in a puff of dust. The torch barely lit a fraction of the huge space below, although Greg could just make out a few broken stone walls. They formed two right angles near the torch, like the corners of urban homes along a sidewalk.

"What is that?" Greg asked.

"I think," Aramis replied, "we've found an entire city underneath Paris."

Athos had far more trouble that he'd expected getting to the city's eastern gate.

The streets were filled with panicked Parisians who were all going in the opposite direction. They were fleeing, fearing the wall was about to be breached by the enemy. Athos had to fight against the rush, ducking into alleys multiple times to avoid being trampled.

When he finally reached the gate, he found the king's guard just as disorganized as the general public.

Despite the chaos, it took Athos only a few seconds to figure out what had happened. There had been a storeroom full of ammunition and gunpowder just north of the gate. Condé's men appeared to have attacked this first and blown it up. The explosion had severely damaged the city wall and thrown the guards into disarray. The fire still blazed; no one had done anything to fight it, and it had spread from the wall to the homes nearby, adding to the bedlam in the streets.

The city wall still stood north of the gate, although Athos could tell it was in bad shape, teetering like a house of cards. One good strike from a battering ram might bring it down. The king's guard had abandoned their posts on it, rightfully fearing it might collapse with them atop it, but now no one was in position to repel the army gathered outside.

The drawbridge that normally should have sealed off the entrance to the city had fallen—although, thankfully, the portcullis was still in place. The thick steel grate was the only thing keeping Condé's army from flooding into the streets. Athos glanced toward the winch that controlled it, expecting to see the king's guard protecting it with their lives. Instead, he spotted four of Condé's men there.

The men had already begun winching the portcullis up. It was hard work—usually a team of horses worked the winch to hoist the massive portcullis—but the men had already raised it a few inches. Outside the gate, Condé's army was pressed against the portcullis, whooping with excitement, eager to stream beneath it and take the city.

Where was Henri? Athos wondered. Who was in command here?

He could find none of the king's guard in the streets, however. So he turned to the few fleeing Parisians left. "Countrymen, I need your help! We must hold off Condé!" With that, he charged Condé's men.

The enemy foursome laughed when they saw him coming. Athos had no uniform. He simply looked like a boy with a sword. Only one man turned to face him, expecting to dispatch him quickly. Instead, Athos made quick work of him. Within seconds, the man was sprawled on the ground—and now Athos had *his* sword as well.

Now the remaining three abandoned the winch, letting the portcullis drop back to the ground. They came at Athos as one, swords gleaming in the firelight. They were all big men, but that simply made them slower in a sword fight. On a normal day, Athos could have defeated them all with ease. But today, his leg was still recovering and he'd already been using it far too much. He didn't have the strength or agility he usually did. Instead, the best he could do was fend off the three swords while his attackers forced him backward across the square.

Behind them, Athos saw more of Condé's men appear from the shadows and race to the winch. There was nothing he could do to stop them. He didn't even think he could handle the three men coming at him. They were pushing him perilously close to the blazing fire. He could feel the heat from it searing the skin on the back of his neck.

Two of Condé's men attacked him in concert, each knocking a blade from his hand. The third brought his sword back with a laugh, preparing to run Athos through.

Suddenly, someone hit him from behind. The man rose up out of the darkness and clobbered Condé's soldier on the head with something heavy. The soldier collapsed, and before the other two could even react, they were assaulted by two other men. As the soldiers dropped, unconscious, Athos could see his saviors' faces in the firelight.

They were three men he'd never seen before. They were merely normal Parisian men who had answered his call to arms. All held blacksmith tools, which they'd used to fight the enemy.

"Thanks," Athos said.

"We're just trying to save our city," one said.

Beyond them, Condé's soldiers had begun to raise the portcullis again. The steel spikes at the bottom emerged from the slots in the ground. On the other side of it, the front ranks of Condé's army were ready to scurry beneath it the moment they had the chance.

"The winch!" Athos cried. He snatched his sword off the street and charged. His newfound warriors came with him. Now, as a team, they quickly took out Condé's men. The winch unspooled once again, and the portcullis slammed back to earth.

When all Condé's men lay at his feet, Athos found that even more Parisians had come forward to answer his call. They had stopped their flight and grabbed whatever they could use as weapons: tools, kitchen knives, farming implements. "What do we do now?" one asked.

"First, sever the rope that controls the portcullis," Athos commanded. "Condé may have more men inside the city, and we don't want anyone lifting that gate."

Three men dutifully set about cutting the rope.

"Next, we need people to take positions on the wall," Athos said. "Not on the weakened part, of course, but there are still some sturdy areas around that and south of the gate. Condé's army will surely be planning to attack the weak spot, and we'll need to fight them off with whatever we have."

"But all the army's weapons were destroyed when the ammunition shed blew," a blacksmith protested.

"Then we must use whatever we can find," Athos said. "We'll throw rocks and stones if we have to. Get the flaming debris from the burning homes and rain that down on the enemy. See if we can set their battering rams on fire."

The Parisians nodded and went to work.

Athos heard a groan from close by. To his surprise, he spotted Henri on the ground. His friend was sitting up, looking dazed, his clothes blackened from the fire.

"Henri!" Athos ran to his side and helped him up. "Are you all right?"

"Yes," Henri replied. "I was trying to guard the ammunition shed, but they got the jump on me. I must have been thrown clear by the blast." He gasped, seeing the aftermath of the explosion. "My men! Where are they?"

"I think they all fled," Athos replied.

"Cowards!" Henri spat.

"But I have found some reinforcements." Athos pointed to the civilians who were now climbing onto the sturdy parts of the wall, armed with stones and rubble.

Henri shook his head. "Regular men and women armed with rocks won't be able to hold off that army for long. Our wall is about to come down. It probably won't take Condé more than an hour to breach it."

"Then we'll hold it as long as we can." Athos worriedly glanced back toward Notre Dame. Whatever Greg and Aramis hoped to do, they now had less than an hour to do it.

 # FIFTEEN

THE RUINS OF THE UNDERGROUND CITY WERE SURPRIS-
ingly large.

Greg, his parents, and Aramis had found a ladder and
climbed down through the hole they'd smashed beneath
the bust of King Louis. All of them held torches, but the
light barely made a dent in the giant cavern where they
stood. Greg had expected they would find one building,
perhaps two beneath them. But they now stood in the
ruins of an entire ancient city.

The streets and buildings of Paris were above their heads

now, as though the city was the first floor of a giant house and a whole Roman city lay in the basement. Modern Paris—or at least this section of it—was supported by a vast network of pilings and columns.

The ancient, subterranean Paris was amazingly well preserved. Most of the roofs had collapsed, but almost everything else remained. The walls of homes and stores still stood. There were streets and sidewalks laid out in a neat, simple grid pattern. Gaps in the streets revealed that clay pipes ran under them, the remnants of an ancient sewer system. The ruins stretched away into the shadows, appearing to go on forever.

"How could all this be here?" Greg asked.

"This is the way old civilizations worked," his father explained. "They just built one city on top of the old one. Paris originally began as a Roman outpost called Lutetia, which was built on this very island because it was easy to defend. However, cities in the middle of rivers tend to flood, and a few hundred years ago, the Parisians realized they needed to shore up their banks. So they raised the city above the ruins here and then built on top of them."

To his surprise, Greg had never realized how high Paris was built above the Seine. Even in 1615, Notre Dame perched a good two stories above the water. In twenty-first-century Paris, the river was flanked by steep walls for miles, as though in a man-made canyon, while the city sat high above the waterline. It had never occurred to him that there might be something *below* the city before. "Why didn't they just fill all this in with dirt and build the city on that?" Greg asked. "Wouldn't that have been sturdier?"

"Not necessarily," his father replied. "Plus, it would have required an incredible amount of dirt in a time well before there were dump trucks to move it."

"In our time, you can actually visit these exact ruins," his mother added. "There's an underground museum across the street from Notre Dame. We were going to take you there."

"Looks like we get to visit for free now," Dad said with a chuckle.

"Can anyone see any place that the other half of the stone might be hidden?" Greg asked.

"I can see a *thousand* places where it might be hidden," Aramis said sourly. "These ruins could cover the entire island."

"No, it must be close," Greg said. "Why else would Dinicoeur say it was *under* the king's nose?"

"Because the entrance to the ruins is under the king's nose," Aramis answered. "That's all he was talking about. As for the stone, it could be *anywhere* down here."

Greg sighed. As usual, nothing concerning the Devil's Stone was ever easy. "How about a Crown of Minerva?" he asked. "The stone ought to be near that. Does anyone see it? Or know where to start looking for it?"

"I don't see any crown around here," Dad replied.

"Neither do I," Aramis said.

"Minerva was the Roman goddess of wisdom, medicine, and commerce," Mom told them. "I'd guess we'd find statues of her near the market, which would have been at the center of a Roman city."

"That would probably be a rectangle marked by a series of evenly spaced columns," Dad put in. "I'm sure some of those must still be standing."

Greg looked to his parents, impressed. Sometimes he forgot how much they knew.

"Any idea how to find that in all this darkness?" Aramis asked.

"As a matter of fact, I do," Dad replied. "I'll be right back!" He scrambled back up the ladder through the hole in the ceiling.

Greg heard him clattering around in the atelier above for a bit, and then he was back. "Help me with this!" he called.

He was lowering something through the hole. Greg and Aramis helped ease it down to the ground. It was a large mirror, its surface chipped and pitted, but it still worked. The light from the torches reflected off it and bounced farther into the ruins.

"I know mirrors aren't too common these days," Dad said, climbing down through the hole again, "but I figured a sculptor would probably have one to help him see his work from all angles."

"Nice thinking, Dad," Greg said.

They angled the mirror to reflect the light around the ruins. Sure enough, toward the center of the island, they spotted a rectangle of broken columns.

"That's it!" Aramis cried.

They quickly picked their way through the ruins to the ancient marketplace. The subterranean city was like a ghost town and a dark, spooky cavern combined. Outside the dim reach of the torches everyone carried, there was only darkness. Anything—or anyone—could be out there. Greg realized he wasn't the only one who felt ill at ease. Everyone stayed clustered together, a small outpost of torchlight in a sea of darkness.

The marketplace was only a shadow of what it had once been. None of the stately columns was intact; most lay toppled and shattered in the dust. Many appeared to have been pilfered to form the pilings supporting the city above.

"I think we need to split up," Dad said. "This place is much bigger than I expected, and we need to work as quickly as possible."

Everyone reluctantly spread out in the darkness to hunt for the Crown of Minerva. Greg's feeling of unease grew worse the farther away from the others he got. It was easy to imagine his enemies lurking in the darkness close by. Surely there were other entrances to this underground world besides the one he'd come through. Dinicoeur or Richelieu could be only a few feet away and he'd never know until their hands were clenched around his neck.

Greg gulped, trying to steady his nerves, and picked carefully through the ruins, keeping one eye out for trouble.

Ahead, he spotted something massive, a sheer wall where the ruins stopped abruptly. He realized it was probably Notre Dame. The cathedral was too massive to simply prop atop pilings like most other buildings. Instead, its foundation had been laid on solid ground, right in the midst of the ancient Roman city.

"Over here!" Mom called.

Greg spun around. His mother was waving her torch excitedly. She was at the far end of the marketplace, and in the gloom, her flame looked as small as a firefly in the distance. The torches of Aramis and Greg's father were already converging on hers.

Greg raced back, relieved to be able to regroup, leaping over toppled columns and crunching through minefields of broken pottery. He found the others gathered in the remains of a large building that had dominated one end of the marketplace. Wide marble steps rose up to it, as though it had been of some importance. The columns that flanked this building—or at least, what remained of them—were far more ornate than those of the rest of the market. The floors were tiled with intricate mosaics, so well preserved that they looked as though they had only been created the day before.

"What was this place?" Greg asked. "A bank?"

"No, someplace far more important to the Romans," his

father replied. "A bathhouse. Most of the rooms around us were used for cleansing." He pointed to places where the floor had collapsed, revealing stacks of what looked like tiles underneath. "That would have been a caldarium—a hot bath. Hot air would have been pumped under the floor there to heat the room."

"Did you find—?" Greg began.

"There," Mom said, pointing with her torch.

Not far away, another intricate mosaic covered an interior wall of the bath. It featured a beautiful woman with long, flowing hair and brilliant blue eyes. She wore a toga and sandals. An owl perched on her shoulder, and a quiver of arrows was slung across her back.

"Minerva," Greg said.

"Yes," Aramis said. "Although there's something strange about that portrait, isn't there?"

"You're right," Greg's father said. "Although I can't put my finger on it, exactly."

"It's not the portrait that's unusual," Greg said. "It's the *wall*."

"What do you mean?" Aramis asked.

"It's *still standing*," Greg explained. "Every other wall in this entire ruin has crumbled at least a little. This one's been built to last."

"And look at this," Greg's mother said. "It's not the only one."

As everyone came closer, they realized that the portrait

of Minerva was actually the front face of a medium-sized room, about twenty feet on each side. Each of the four walls was equally well built and still standing after almost two millennia. All were covered with intricate mosaics depicting Minerva.

"Whoever built this certainly wanted it to stand the test of time," Dad said. He rapped his knuckles against it. "These walls feel like they're a foot thick."

"And there's no door," Aramis said. "It seems to be a crypt of some sort."

"To hold the Devil's Stone," Greg said. Even as he spoke the words, he knew they were true. He could feel the stone he wore around his own neck pulsing more now. It actually seemed to be pulling him toward the crypt, as though both halves of the stone were attracted to each other.

"But how are we supposed to get to it if there's no door?" Mom asked.

"That's for us to figure out, I think," Dad told her. "It wasn't supposed to be easy to get to this half."

"We need to find the Crown of Minerva," Greg said. He returned his attention to the first mosaic they'd encountered. The very top of Minerva's head was obscured by a cloud of ancient cobwebs. Greg brushed it away and, to his delight, found a crown hidden behind them—a bejeweled tiara studded with opalescent stones. His joy quickly turned to frustration, however. He'd been hoping the next part would be easy—that there might be an inscription on the crown, telling them what to do next—but now he realized they were stuck again.

"Maybe it's the wrong Minerva," his mother said.

Greg's father and Aramis quickly circled the crypt to examine the other portraits of Minerva. "No," Dad reported sadly. "None of the others is wearing a crown."

"So what do we do now?" Aramis asked Greg. "Can you make the half of the stone you already have do something to make the crypt open?"

"Like what?" Greg asked.

"I don't know," Aramis said. "If the stone gives you all sorts of power, maybe you can just *wish* the crypt to open or something."

Greg didn't think that would work, but he tried it anyhow, just to make sure. He focused all his concentration on the crypt, willing the walls to crumble—or slide aside—or do *something*. But they stayed stubbornly upright.

Greg shook his head with a sigh. They couldn't have come all this way, come so close, just to get stymied now. "The stone won't do this for us," he said. "We have to do it ourselves, to prove our worth. I know there's a solution. I can sense it somehow. It's like all the pieces of the puzzle are there, but I just can't figure out how to put them together. . . ."

He found his eye drawn to the the glittering jewels in Minerva's crown. While most of them were nice, uniform geometric shapes like squares and diamonds, the one in the center was oddly asymmetrical. And yet there was something strangely familiar about it. Greg stared at it a moment, wondering where he'd seen it before, his own words echoing in his head. *All the pieces of the puzzle . . . figure out how to put them together.*

He gasped, suddenly realizing where he'd seen the shape before. "It all makes sense."

"What?" Aramis asked.

"The answer has been right in front of me all along," Greg said. He lifted the amulet from around his neck and stood on tiptoe before the mosaic. The half of the Devil's Stone in his hand and the jewel in the center of the crown were exactly the same size and shape.

The others gasped in recognition.

Greg popped the stone out of the amulet, then pressed it into the matching spot on the mosaic. The tile retracted into the wall and the stone locked into place with a click.

Nothing else happened.

It simply remained eerily quiet in the ruins.

"What now?" Greg asked.

"You've only put the key in the lock," Aramis told him. "Maybe you still have to turn it."

Greg set his hand on the stone. To his surprise, it turned easily. There were more clicks from behind the wall, as if turning the stone had set off a chain of events, each bigger than the last. The clicks grew louder and louder, and the crypt rumbled as though some ancient machinery inside was coming to life.

The ground trembled. Dust fell from the ceiling. And then an ancient doorway in the crypt wall slid open with a gasp of stale air.

Greg popped his half of the Devil's Stone free from the mosaic. The door stayed open, and Greg and the others rushed into the crypt to see what they'd found.

The room was simply designed on the inside. The walls, floor, and ceiling were lined with marble, as much of Paris and Rome had once been. Only here, thieves had never been able to get in to steal it all.

In the center of the room a beautiful statue of Minerva sculpted in marble stood on a pedestal. Another silver amulet hung around her neck, and in the center of it sat the second half of the Devil's Stone.

The pedestal was so high, Greg needed a boost to get on top of it. His father had to help him up. There were some words in Latin engraved in the pedestal:

AD OMNEM QUI UTET SAXUM. CAVE.
NOSCE DIFFERENTIAM INTER QUOD CUPIS
ET QUOD EGES.

"What does that mean?" Greg asked.

"'To all who would use the stone, beware,'" Aramis translated. "'Know the difference between what you desire and what you need.'"

"Sounds like good advice," Mom said.

Balanced atop the pedestal, Greg grasped the chain that held the amulet around Minerva's neck. It had been so difficult to get to this point, he expected that the chain would be locked to the statue somehow—or that the stone would turn out to be only a hologram—or that some other test would arise. Instead, the chain lifted off easily, and suddenly, after so much time, energy, and adventure, Greg finally had both stones in his possession.

He could feel them pull toward each other now. The room seemed to surge with power.

He would have put them together right then and there, except that he had to free the second stone from its amulet. He couldn't do that while standing on the pedestal, so he hopped back down to the marble floor. . . .

Only to feel a dark shadow fall over him.

"Hand over the stones," said Michel Dinicoeur.

Dinicoeur and Richelieu both stood in the doorway to the crypt. Richelieu held two torches. Dinicoeur stood behind Aramis, a knife to the boy's neck. "If you even attempt to put those stones together, I will kill him," he snarled.

Greg held up each half of the stone separately so his enemies could see them. "Take the knife away from his neck," he ordered.

Dinicoeur did so, though he kept the blade close.

"Here," Greg said, and flung both stones over the heads

of Dinicoeur and Richelieu and out the door of the crypt.

His enemies gasped and whirled after them.

Greg was hoping to get the jump on them at this point, but Dinicoeur shoved Aramis into Greg, and both boys tumbled to the floor. Dinicoeur and Richelieu slipped out of the crypt. Greg's parents raced after them, but before they could get out, the great stone door closed, locking them inside.

It slammed shut with a great gust of air that snuffed out the torches, leaving Greg and his family trapped in the darkness—with both halves of the Devil's Stone on the other side.

Porthos and Catherine made it into the Louvre without any trouble. Now that the city was under siege, the king's guard was nowhere to be seen. Some had raced off to man the defenses. Others had fled in fear. None had stayed to protect the palace. Porthos and Catherine walked right through the front doors.

Once inside, however, they still thought it best to stay out of sight. Catherine went directly to the first access to the secret passages she knew of—a sliding panel just off the grand entry hall—and from there they wound their way through the labyrinth of hidden tunnels. As they finally moved quickly up the spiral staircase to Milady's lair, Porthos was huffing and puffing with exertion.

Catherine paused on the landing. The door was open a

crack, although she thought she'd shut it before leaving. She turned to Porthos, about to say something, but he signaled her to stay quiet and unsheathed his sword. Then he flung the door open and leaped into the room, ready for battle.

No one attacked, however.

The room was empty. The ropes that Catherine and Greg's parents had used to tie up Milady, Condé, and Condé's men lay on the floor, sliced to pieces.

"They've escaped!" Catherine gasped.

"Take me to the king's quarters immediately," Porthos told her. "They're going to kill him."

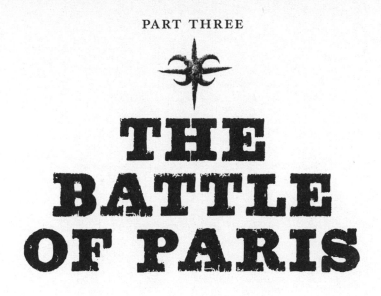

PART THREE

THE
BATTLE
OF PARIS

☩— SIXTEEN

TRAPPED IN THE DARK IN THE CRYPT, IT TOOK EVERY ounce of self-control Greg had not to panic. Panic wouldn't solve his problems. If anything, it would make them worse. You breathed faster when you panicked, and there was only so much air in the crypt. If he wanted to figure a way out of here, he needed to stay calm and keep focused.

The problem was, he needed to figure out a way *fast*. It wasn't for his own safety—there was probably enough air to last everyone an hour—but because Dinicoeur and Richelieu were on the outside with both halves of the Devil's

Stone. Hopefully, the pieces wouldn't be easy to find, lying somewhere in the ruins in the dark, but there was a chance they had landed right out in the open as well.

Greg's mother began to wail in fear. "We're trapped!" she cried.

"It will be all right," Greg's father told her reassuringly, although Greg could hear the panic at the edge of his voice as well. The two of them had been traumatized by being locked in a dark prison cell in La Mort. This was the perfect scenario to bring all that horror right back.

Greg carefully made his way through the dark to the front of the crypt, where the door was—or at least, where he *thought* it was. Perhaps the door really hadn't locked them in. Perhaps there was a way to open it from the inside. But it wasn't going to be that easy. The door might as well have been a wall. It didn't budge when he shoved against it.

He could hear the muffled voices of Dinicoeur and Richelieu on the other side, bickering as they searched for the halves of the Devil's Stone.

"I can't see them anywhere!" Richelieu cried.

"Don't use your eyes to look for them," Dinicoeur ordered. "Try to sense them. The stones have power you can feel. . . . Aha! Here's one now!"

A hand suddenly clamped on Greg's wrist, startling him.

"Don't worry," Aramis said. "It's only me. Do you still have any matches left?"

"Only one," Greg said. "I've been saving it for an emergency."

"I think this qualifies," Aramis replied. "Let's pray it works. We need it to light this grenade."

With that, he pressed a large steel ball into Greg's hand.

"How did you . . . ?" Greg began.

"It's one of Dinicoeur's," Aramis replied. "He had a pouch full of them. While he was busy holding a knife to my neck, I swiped one."

Greg fumbled the oil skin out of the purse on his belt and carefully unwrapped the match. "Mom! Dad! Get behind the pedestal!" he ordered.

As they maneuvered in the dark, Greg found the wick on the grenade. It wasn't very long. He'd have only a few seconds to get to cover. "It'll do more damage if we can find a crevice in the wall to set it in," he told Aramis.

"All right," Aramis said, then ran his hands along the wall until he found a good-sized gap in the stone. "I've got one!" he cried. "There's a groove here on the edge where the door meets the wall."

Greg followed Aramis's voice and found the groove himself. "Okay," he said. "Now you go take cover, too."

"No . . ."

"There's no time to argue. Just go."

Greg listened to Aramis race back to the pedestal.

On the other side of the door, he heard Richelieu cry out, "I can sense the other half! It's over here somewhere."

Greg pinched his one remaining match in his fingers. *Please work,* he prayed.

He struck it along the wall.

It lit. In the pitch darkness, even the small, sudden flare of light was almost blinding. Greg carefully touched the match to the wick of the grenade.

The flame sputtered . . . and quickly burned out.

Greg sucked in a breath, terrified. "No," he whispered. He heard both his parents gasp as fear set in again. Even Aramis wailed, "No! No . . ."

Greg looked down at the grenade, unable to believe what had happened.

And there, he saw it. A tiny red glow in the darkness, like the embers of a fire. The end of the wick *had* caught, just barely.

Greg cautiously lifted the grenade to his face and carefully breathed on the wick, trying to give the tiny ember a bit more oxygen without blowing it out entirely.

The red glow grew. And then the wick *really* caught, sparking and smoking.

"It's going!" Greg shouted. He crammed the grenade into the groove between the door and the wall of the crypt and raced to safety.

The tiny light of the wick was enough to illuminate the room, and the statue of Minerva flickered in the dim glow. Greg slid across the marble floor and ducked down behind the pedestal.

"There it is!" Richelieu cried on the other side of the wall. "I see the other half!"

The grenade exploded.

The blast was incredibly loud in the tiny crypt, and for a moment, it was as bright as day. Greg huddled tightly with the others behind the pedestal as huge pieces of stone flew past and caromed off the walls. The air filled with the acrid stench of burnt gunpowder.

Once Greg sensed the worst of the debris had flown past, he chanced standing up from behind the pedestal. The statue of Minerva had been sheared off just above his head. Now, only her feet remained on the pedestal. The rest of the beautiful statue was gone.

Through the smoke, Greg could see the glimmer of torches out in the ruins. There was no longer a wall between him and his enemies, only a gaping hole.

"We did it!" Aramis cried.

Greg was already racing out of the crypt. "Come on! There's no time to celebrate."

He emerged through the hole to find Dinicoeur and Richelieu down for the count. The grenade had blown most of the debris out toward them, catching them by surprise. A huge rock had caught Dinicoeur in the chest and knocked him flat. He lay on his back, struggling to get out from under it, the first half of the Devil's Stone lying on the ground just out of his reach. Richelieu lay sprawled unconscious in a field of stones twenty yards away.

Greg snatched the first half of the stone away from Dinicoeur's hands. Dinicoeur roared in hatred, his eyes glowing red in the firelight. "Give that back, you fool!"

"Never again," Greg told him.

He turned back toward the crypt, expecting the others to have joined him by now. "Is something wrong?" he asked.

"Your father's leg is caught under a piece of debris," Aramis replied. "He's fine, but it's taking us a while to get him free."

"I'll be right there," Greg called back. "I just need to find the other half of the stone."

He didn't try looking for it. As Dinicoeur suggested to Richelieu, he tried sensing it. Sure enough, with one half of the stone clutched in his hand, he could feel the power of the other close by. He tried to home in on it, letting the stone pull him along.

He paused near the prone body of Richelieu, the man who would become Dinicoeur—and thus, the man who had caused him so much misery. *I could end it now,* he thought. Richelieu's sword lay nearby. In just a few seconds, Greg could slice the man's neck. If Richelieu died before attaining immortality, then Dinicoeur's existence would be negated as well.

But Greg couldn't bring himself to do it. He couldn't kill a defenseless man, no matter how evil he was.

Then he saw the stone. It was still fastened into the amulet that had hung around the statue's neck, lying in the dust only a few feet away from Richelieu. Greg eagerly raced toward it, trying to control his excitement. He scrambled through the ruins and bent down to pick it up. . . .

When Richelieu suddenly attacked.

Greg heard the blade slicing through the air before he saw it. He spun away just as the sword crashed down.

Stupid, Greg told himself. Richelieu hadn't been unconscious. He'd merely been lying in wait. Greg had dropped his guard and hadn't even thought to arm himself.

Richelieu came at him again. Greg dodged the blade and lunged for the only handy thing to defend himself—a torch lying nearby. He tumbled across the ground and grabbed it, spinning to meet Richelieu's next attack, though as he did, the first half of the Devil's Stone slipped from his hand and fell into the dirt near the second.

There wasn't time to pick them up. Greg deflected Richelieu's slash with the torch, creating a shower of sparks. Richelieu came again and again, backing Greg through the ruins. Greg blocked the sword with the torch each time, but the wood was splintering apart beneath the steel. The sparks that flew off stung Greg's eyes and singed his skin.

"Aramis!" he yelled. "I need some help here!"

"I'm coming!" Aramis yelled back, although his voice was far away, across the ruins.

Greg's torch was almost reduced to matchsticks. He didn't think it would last until Aramis got there.

Richelieu stabbed at him, and Greg felt a rush of pain as the sword nicked his side. Richelieu swung the sword out, bringing it around toward Greg's head. . . .

And Greg saw his opening. He brought the torch down on Richelieu's arm.

Richelieu screamed as the fire seared his skin, and he dropped his sword.

Greg snatched the weapon before it could even hit the ground and turned it on its owner. He slashed toward Richelieu, and saw his opponent gasp in terror. . . .

Greg froze in mid-swing, his sword pressed against the flesh of Richelieu's neck, unable even now to kill the man. "On your knees," he ordered.

Richelieu nodded, amazed that Greg had spared his life. His eyes were still wide with fear.

Although Greg noticed them flick to focus on something behind him.

"D'Artagnan!" Aramis yelled. "Look out!"

Greg was moving before his friend could finish his warning, sensing something terrible was coming. He whirled around to find Dinicoeur charging toward him. The madman had freed himself and recovered his sword. Now he'd clearly planned to kill Greg from behind.

As Greg spun, the blade just missed him. Dinicoeur hurtled past, stunned that he'd missed his target and now unable to stop his own momentum.

The sword intended for Greg plunged into Richelieu's chest, stabbing him right through the heart.

It happened so quickly, Richelieu didn't even seem

to feel the pain of it. He staggered backward, staring in astonishment at the sword jutting from his body, and then looked up at Dinicoeur. "You fool," he gasped. "You've killed us."

He stumbled again and fell to the ground. Taking one last breath, he died.

Now Dinicoeur screamed. It was a howl of agony and frustration, of four centuries of pent-up rage. He grabbed a large stone off the ground and came at Greg, his eyes wild with fury. "You insufferable wretch!" he roared. "I'll bash your head in!"

Greg scrambled away through the ruins.

Dinicoeur tried to follow, but a change was coming over him. He seemed to be fading; Greg could see things faintly through the madman's body. The heavy stone dropped through his hands. Dinicoeur watched his arm slowly vanishing before his eyes and screamed again. "No! What's happening to me?"

"By killing your younger self, you've negated your own existence," Greg told him.

Dinicoeur gaped at him, horror in his eyes as he realized what he'd done, as he grasped that his four hundred years of misery had ended in failure.

He started to say something but could no longer speak. His body was completely transparent now, like that of a ghost. He was fading quickly, melting into the darkness. In his eyes, Greg saw shock and rage and terror.

And then, Dinicoeur was gone.

Greg stood there for a few moments afterward, staring at the space where Dinicoeur had been, wondering if what he'd seen was possible, trying to comprehend that the horrible madman was truly gone for good.

Aramis was suddenly by his side. "You did it," he said. "You killed him."

"No," Greg said. "He did that himself."

It seemed that he should feel relief, but instead, he knew all was still not right. He felt overwhelmed. The exhaustion that had waned when he held the Devil's Stone now returned with a vengeance, washing over him, as though the stone's force had faded as well.

The stone!

Greg turned toward where he'd last seen the pieces and raced over to recover them. But the ground was bare.

"The halves of the stone are gone!" he cried.

"How?" Aramis asked.

Greg wondered if he was looking in the wrong place. So much of the ruins here looked the same. But no, he could see the mark in the dirt where Richelieu had lain, the scuff marks their battle had left, and . . .

A set of much smaller footprints in the dirt.

In an instant, he realized what had happened. "Milady!" Greg gasped. Milady had known just as much about the location of the stone as he had. She had heard Catherine's story about it being under the king's nose—and she'd taken

Dinicoeur's map with the Crown of Minerva marked on it. For all he knew, she'd followed him down there. Or perhaps she'd followed Dinicoeur. Then all she had to do was lurk in the darkness and wait for her chance. She had swiped the pieces of the stone while he, Richelieu, and Dinicoeur were distracted by their battle. Meaning she couldn't have gone far.

Greg looked across the ruins toward the hole they'd entered through. Sure enough, someone with golden hair in a white dress was scrambling up the ladder through it.

Greg went after her.

 # SEVENTEEN

From atop the eastern wall of Paris, Athos watched the machines of war approaching. Catapults. Trebuchets. Siege towers. Battering rams. He'd seen them only from a distance before. Now they seemed enormous to him. Backlit by the bonfires and torches of Condé's army, the huge wooden structures looked like beasts from another world.

Each sat on a wooden base with wheels a yard in diameter. They were so big, they required dozens of men to move each one, but still, they came. Condé's army slowly rolled them toward the wall, using them for both the assault and protection. The war machines were covered with metal plates, which shielded everyone behind them from attack. The rest of the army followed the machines, a thousand men strong, waiting until the walls of Paris crumbled and they could surge into the city. There were so many torches in the darkness, it was like looking into a star-filled sky.

Athos had virtually nothing—and no one—to fight back with. He and Henri had managed to round up ten members of the king's guard, who now stood with Athos. These men had swords, bows, and a few arrows each. In addition to them, some brave and stalwart citizens had joined them, determined to do whatever it took to defend the city, but they had only tools and rubble to fight with. The entire force was less than forty people. Against Condé's massive army and its war machines, they were like David facing Goliath.

The catapults and trebuchets were massive levers, designed to hurl heavy objects at the walls—or over them. They could take more than an hour to load and fire, but the damage they could do was extraordinary. Over the past day, many buildings close to the city walls had been reduced to rubble from the massive boulders flung by these machines. Now Condé's army had come up with something even worse: They were coating their loads in pitch and then setting them on fire.

The result was huge, flaming projectiles. The army had

already launched one. It had screamed over the wall like a comet, decimated a church, and set an entire block of the city on fire. Athos had ordered the citizens of Paris to form a bucket brigade to the river before the rest of the city went up in flames. They were working hard at it now, but so many people were fighting the fire, there were almost none left to defend the city.

Now, not far away, another trebuchet was loaded. A stone the size of a church bell dangled in the sling at the end of its lever, waiting to be whipped into the air. Athos could see the army painting it with pitch.

"We don't have enough people to fight another fire," Henri confided. "If that comes over, the whole city could burn down."

"Then we'll need to fight fire with fire," Athos replied. He ordered the ten members of the king's guard along the wall to dip their arrows in pitch and set them ablaze. At his command, all of them fired on the trebuchet.

Eight arrows missed their targets. The ninth, however, struck the barrel full of pitch the enemy was gathered around. It went up in flames, setting the clothes of the men around it on fire, sending them screaming for the river. The tenth arrow severed the rope that held the sling. The huge rock tumbled free, and the trebuchet's lever, suddenly relieved of its payload, whipped forward with such force that it tore the entire machine apart.

A cheer went up from the men on the wall. Henri patted Athos on the shoulder proudly. "Well done!" he crowed.

Athos barely allowed himself a moment of joy, however. There was more trouble on the horizon, and it wouldn't be nearly as easy to take care of.

The siege towers were extremely simple in concept: mobile towers designed to be rolled right up to the city walls, allowing the enemy to come over the top. Each was twenty feet tall, and the fronts had been faced with iron plates. The Parisian army's arrows bounced off them harmlessly.

The walls of Paris had been designed to thwart siege towers: There was a four-foot trench around the city to prevent anything from being wheeled directly to the wall. But Condé's men had come up with a devious addition: a tiny drawbridge at the top of each tower. Now the towers could be parked at the far edge of the moat, and the drawbridge could be dropped to the top of the city wall. Once that happened, the enemy would be able to stream over the ramparts; Athos didn't have enough men to hold them off.

And even if he could stop the siege towers, there were still the battering rams to worry about. These, too, were extremely simple: A huge tree trunk was suspended from a wooden frame and capped with a pointed iron tip. When swung, the ram would slam into the wall with great force. One was now being moved into place at the point where the city wall was weakest. One solid shot from that, Athos figured, and the wall would come tumbling down.

Once again, there was nothing he could do to stop it. Condé's men had cleverly roofed the battering ram with iron plates, providing themselves with a giant shield umbrella beneath which they could move about without any fear of being hit by arrows.

Not that Athos had many arrows left anyhow. He was running out. In fact, he was running out of everything. When Condé's men had detonated the ammunition shed, the French soldiers had lost almost all their weapons. Some of them were down to pelting the invading army below with rocks.

Still, Athos kept his post, not wanting to cede victory until the very last moment. As long as he stayed, Henri would stay, and as long as Henri was there, the soldiers would stay, too. Athos set another arrow on fire and loosed it at the approaching siege tower, hoping there was a way to set it aflame. Instead, the precious arrow clanged off the iron plates and fell to the ground, where it was instantly snuffed beneath the tower's wheels. Athos sighed; it was like trying to defeat a dragon.

"How much longer do you think we have?" Henri asked.

"Not long at all," Athos replied.

"Then why continue risking our men's lives? Perhaps Condé will spare us in defeat."

"No. We need to stay here. We need every second of defense we can buy this city."

"But the city is going to fall," Henri argued. "The only thing that can save it is a miracle."

"Yes." Athos glanced back toward the center of the city, wondering what was happening with the rest of the Musketeers. "A miracle is exactly what we are waiting for."

Catherine and Porthos raced through the network of hidden passages in the palace. Porthos felt like a rat running through a maze. Some of the tunnels were so narrow he could barely squeeze his considerable bulk through them. "I need to go on a diet," he puffed. "How close can these tunnels get us to the king's quarters?"

"They can get us *into* the king's quarters," Catherine replied.

"Oh no," Porthos said. Normally, the king's bedchamber would have been barricaded and guarded. But if the enemy was already in the tunnels, they could get around that.

"These tunnels were designed so the king could *escape* attackers," Catherine explained. "I don't think it ever occurred to anyone what might happen if the attackers used the tunnels themselves."

"And I suspect Milady knows all the ins and outs of

them." Porthos sighed.

"Information that Condé no doubt knows as well. Here we are." Catherine stopped by an ordinary-looking panel and threw a hidden latch. The panel swung open, revealing the bedroom of King Louis . . . and four assassins. Condé and his men were gathered around the ornate blue canopy bed where Louis slept, unaware that death was seconds away. Milady wasn't there, although Porthos and Catherine had no time to speculate where she might be. They'd arrived just in time. Condé was removing a dagger from its sheath.

"Your Majesty!" Porthos shouted. "Look out!"

Louis snapped awake, and from across the room Porthos could see the king's eyes go wide with terror. At the same time, however, Porthos had caught Condé and his men by surprise. They turned toward the door, startled by the intrusion, giving Louis time to spring away.

Condé lunged for the king, but he was too late. His dagger plunged into the bed instead.

One of his men caught Louis before he could get away. He tried to wrestle the king down so Condé could have another go at him.

Meanwhile, the other two men came toward Porthos and Catherine, swords at the ready.

Porthos screamed at the top of his lungs and charged. In truth, he really had no idea what else to do. He merely hoped that yelling and attacking like a crazy person would at least give his enemies some pause, if not scare them out of their boots.

It worked. Porthos could scream in a very frightening way, and when his entire bulk was coming at a person full force, waving a sword, it was quite terrifying. Condé's men hesitated, and that was just long enough for Porthos to barrel into them. They tumbled back onto the bed, which collapsed under their weight, and the canopy dropped over them, shrouding them in darkness.

Their heads were easy to spot, poking up under the canopy, and Porthos slammed them together with such force that the crack sounded like a gunshot. The men collapsed beneath him.

Meanwhile, Condé's other man had overwhelmed Louis, and now held the king's arms while Condé himself raised his dagger for another shot.

Porthos scrambled to help the king, but he wasn't fast enough.

As Condé attacked, though, Louis lifted his feet off the floor and delivered a two-footed kick to Condé's chest that sent him sprawling. Then he whipped his head back, slamming it into the nose of the man behind him. The man howled, releasing his grip, and Louis pulled free.

Two swords hung on the wall. Porthos had assumed they were for decoration, but now Louis yanked them off and whipped the air with them.

"Your Majesty!" Porthos gasped. "You know how to fight?"

"Of course I do!" Louis shot back. "What do you think, I just sit on my throne all day?"

Condé now pulled out his own sword. Porthos met the attack, while Louis fended off Condé's man. Beneath the canopy, the other two soldiers were beginning to stir again, but Catherine set upon them with the only weapon she could find: the king's chamber pot. It was a large ceramic tub, there so the king wouldn't have to leave his room to relieve himself at night. Thankfully, it was empty, and it was a very effective blunt instrument. Catherine cracked her enemies hard enough on their heads to break the tub in half, and both sagged into unconsciousness again.

Condé and his remaining man were trouble, however. Porthos and Louis did their best to battle them, but both of the enemy were quite adept with their swords. Porthos found himself overmatched. He was exhausted from running across the city as it was, and now he was thinking that he probably should have been practicing his sword fighting a bit more instead of teasing Athos and Greg for how much they practiced.

It wasn't long before Condé knocked the sword from his hand, leaving him defenseless. Porthos had no choice but to back away as Condé came toward him, grinning cruelly.

"You have failed again, Musketeer," he warned. "The king will still die tonight. And now, you will, too."

Greg clambered through the hole in the atelier floor just in time to see Milady disappearing out the window. He caught a glimpse of the silver chain dangling from her hand, indicating that she hadn't freed the second half of the Devil's Stone from the amulet yet. If she had, no doubt she would have put the pieces together already and used the power to kill him or make herself queen or who knew what else. So he ran after her, determined not to give her the chance.

By the time he reached the window, she was halfway across the plaza toward Notre Dame. As he pursued her, she ducked into the door at the base of the southern bell tower.

Oh no, Greg thought. He'd had a terrible experience in that tower once before.

But he went after her nonetheless. What other choice did he have?

He could hear Milady racing up the bell tower steps when he entered and he started up as well. The railing was just as flimsy as he remembered, and he hadn't gone far up before the steps began to get slick with the droppings of the thousands of pigeons and bats that lived in the belfry. He was aching with exhaustion now, and racing up ten flights of stairs was probably the worst thing he could be doing in his condition. He could barely catch his breath. His heart hammered in his chest. But still, he pushed on.

Milady kept on going up and up and up. Greg knew she wasn't lying in wait for him anywhere because he could hear her pounding the steps above. She reached the landing where the giant bell Emmanuel hung, but to Greg's surprise, she didn't stop there. A thin ladder was built into the side of the tower, and he spotted Milady scurrying up it, so he followed.

He had to sheathe his sword now, needing both hands to climb. He went up into the rafters, past the massive beam that supported Emmanuel, until he reached an open trapdoor at the top. He scrambled through it and found himself in the center of a large, flat square of stone without so much as a safety railing. Below him, to the east, he caught a glimpse of Condé's massive army gathered outside the wall and the fires burning in the city. He spun around, searching for where Milady had gone. . . .

Only to see her coming right at him. Her sword gleamed in the moonlight.

Greg dodged and the blade barely missed him, but he couldn't avoid Milady. She bowled him over, and both tumbled to the edge of the roof. Greg stopped with his head dangling over the precipice, Milady atop him, her face just inches from his. The last time they'd been this close, she'd been batting her eyes at him, acting as though she was entranced by him. Now he saw only cold, murderous hatred in those eyes. Milady clenched one hand around his neck, digging her nails into his flesh, while she tried to shove him over the edge.

Greg struggled to fight back, but his strength was almost gone. Climbing the tower had sapped the last of it. And now Milady had the power of the stones. Even though she hadn't put them together, she was gaining their strength. Her hand was like a vise on Greg's neck, cutting off his air. Soon she would send him off the edge, and he'd plummet to the street far below.

"I thought you wanted to rule the world with me," he gasped. "I thought you wanted me by your side."

"I only said that to get the stone, you fool." Milady's eyes reflected the distant fires, making them seem a devilish red. "But now that I have them, I don't need you or anyone else by my side. I can rule this country on my own!"

Milady started to give Greg the final shove over the edge . . . and then she stopped. Her smile faded, and her eyes now registered surprise.

Greg looked up. The blade of a sword was now pressed against her neck. Aramis stood above her, holding it.

"There's one big problem with only looking out for yourself," the Musketeer said. "You don't have anybody to watch your back. Now help D'Artagnan get to safety."

"Or what?" Milady sneered. "You'll kill me? If you do, he'll drop and die himself."

"I know," Aramis replied. "I have no intention of killing you if you don't comply. Instead, I'll just cause you a great deal of pain. I assume you don't want a hideous scar on that perfect neck of yours." Aramis spoke with a determination neither Greg nor Milady had ever heard in him before. He pressed the sword deeper into her flesh.

Milady winced in response. Her eyes narrowed in anger, but unlike Dinicoeur, she had the presence of mind to control her rage. She pulled Greg back onto the safety of the roof and removed her hand from his neck.

Greg gasped for air, relieved to be alive.

"Now hand D'Artagnan the stones," Aramis demanded. "And know this: Now that he is safe, if you try anything untoward, I *will* kill you."

Milady might have been conniving, duplicitous, and traitorous, but above all else, she valued her own life. Aware that she was beaten, she took the halves of the Devil's Stone and pressed them into Greg's hands.

For a moment, Greg stared at them in amazement, unable to believe that after so long, he finally had both pieces of the Devil's Stone.

He looked to Aramis. "You saved my life," he said.

"Of course," his friend replied. "We're a team. All for one . . ."

". . . and one for all," Greg finished.

And then, from the east came a thunderous crash. Greg spun around. In the light of the fire from the blazing city, he could see that a portion of the city wall had collapsed. Now Condé's men were streaming through the gap into the city.

Paris had fallen.

EIGHTEEN

ATHOS WATCHED FROM THE RAMPARTS AS THE BATTERING ram slammed into the wall. The ground trembled as the stones came tumbling down. A mighty roar went up from Condé's army and the soldiers funneled toward the gap. Athos and his men fired their last arrows, hitting a few of the enemy in the legs and arms and taking them down, but they might as well have been throwing sticks at a tidal wave.

At the same time, on his other flank, a drawbridge dropped from a siege tower onto the top of the wall.

Condé's men streamed over the ramparts.

"Abandon your posts!" Athos yelled, although in truth, the few members of the guard who had stayed this long were already deserting. Athos raced down the steps from the ramparts to the ground.

The opposing army poured into the city, wielding weapons and torches. They swarmed through the wall and over it. Athos tried to sprint for the safety of the alleys of Paris, but his wounded leg finally gave out on him. Pain shot through it, and he tumbled to the cobblestones. No one stopped to help him. Instead, the guards he'd commanded—even Henri—disappeared into the alleys. Athos didn't bear them any ill will, though. He understood: Anyone who stopped for him would fall behind, and falling behind meant death. Condé's men would show no mercy.

Athos rolled over to find the enemy coming at him from all sides. His sword lay on the ground nearby. Even though he could no longer stand, he picked it up and brandished it menacingly. If he was going to die tonight, he would at least take some of the enemy down with him.

He only hoped that his death wouldn't be in vain.

The triumphant roar of Condé's army echoed through Paris. Even all the way across the city, in the bedchamber of King Louis, they could hear it. Everyone glanced out the window toward the eastern wall. They were too far to see the individual men in the darkness, but they could see the light of the enemy torches moving into the city.

Porthos's heart sank. Condé grinned cruelly. He called to King Louis, who was still battling Condé's man. "Put down your sword, cousin! As you can see, there is no longer any point in fighting. Your city has fallen. Your reign is over."

"If you drop that sword, he'll kill you," Porthos warned. "He'll march you out into the town square and make a spectacle of your beheading. It is far better to die with honor."

Condé wheeled back on him, waving the tip of his sword in Porthos's face. "It doesn't matter how much honor you display in this room," he snarled. "The victor is the one who tells the tale. And when people ask how you went, I will tell them you showed no honor at all, that you groveled for your life and cried like a little girl. What do you think of that?"

"To be honest, I'm not too fond of it," Porthos replied. "Let's try something else."

There was a flash of silver, and Condé's sword was knocked from his hand. He spun to find Catherine armed with Porthos's sword, which she now directed at *his* throat.

"For starters, we could see how *you* behave when faced with death," Catherine said.

"Yes," Porthos said. "I like that idea considerably better." With Catherine keeping Condé at bay, he lunged across the room to help the king. Condé's man had Louis backed into a corner, but Porthos blindsided the man and slammed him headfirst into the wall. He groaned in pain and went down in a heap.

"A thousand thanks," Louis said.

"It is my honor, Your Majesty," Porthos replied.

Now that he was on the wrong end of a sword and his men were out of commission, Condé's bravado quickly faded. "Killing me won't solve anything," he said, his voice quavering. "In fact, you need me. My army has taken Paris. Soon, they will mob the castle. The soldiers will tear you all limb from limb unless I tell them to spare your lives."

Porthos, Louis, and Catherine all shared a look of concern. None had intended to kill Condé, but the man had a point nonetheless. Out the window, the flood of torches was now spreading farther into Paris. Even though Louis's life had been spared, it seemed that his rule had come to an end.

"I assure you, you will not die by any of our hands," Louis said diplomatically. "And in return, I ask the same of you. I will abdicate my throne peacefully in return for you sparing the lives of all who have served me."

Condé smiled. "Of course."

"Don't believe him," Porthos warned. "Condé's word is no better than that of a snake. The moment his army gets here, he'll throw us to the dogs."

"What other choice do I have?" Louis asked sadly.

Before Porthos could answer, there was a blinding flash of light atop Notre Dame.

The moment Greg put the two halves of the Devil's Stone together, an incredible surge of energy burst forth from them. He had experienced it once before, in the Louvre, when Michel Dinicoeur had first made the portal to the past, but the sheer power of it still caught him by surprise. It rolled out from the stone like an invisible wave, so strong that it knocked Aramis and Milady off their feet and nearly sent them skidding over the edge of the bell tower.

But that was nothing compared to the power that Greg could now feel *inside* him.

He felt invincible. No, he *knew* he was invincible. Anything he wanted . . . his greatest desire . . . could be his.

If he chose, he could be immortal as Dinicoeur had been. If he wanted, he could be powerful, as Milady had desired. He could almost feel the stone speaking to him, filling his head with ideas about what he could be, the greatness he could have if he harnessed its power. Forget about Louis or Condé. *He* could be the ruler of France. And he could rule it forever, immune to the petty fears of mere mortals. If he wanted, the army below would bow down before him and install him on the throne.

The whole purpose he'd wanted the stone for, the reason he'd sought it—to get back home again—seemed like a foolish idea. A waste of a once-in-a-lifetime opportunity.

What would the point be? If he went back to Queens, he'd only be an anonymous, insignificant, unhappy teenager again. But if he stayed here and used the stone the right way, he could be one of the most powerful men in history. Sure, he might be changing the future of the world, but who cared? Why couldn't *his* name go down in the history books?

Do it, Greg thought, although he wasn't sure whether it was actually himself thinking it or the stone doing it for him. *Make yourself king. Make yourself immortal. Make yourself invincible forever. Your greatest desire will come true.*

Greg opened his mouth, prepared to say the words.

And then he saw Aramis.

His friend was staring at him in fear, as if he *knew* Greg was about to be corrupted by the stone.

Then Greg looked to Milady. She was staring at him with her hypnotic eyes, basking in the power of the stone. She, too, seemed to know what was in his mind, and she certainly approved.

And then Greg looked down to the city beneath him. For the moment, the attack had ceased. The explosion of light atop Notre Dame had grabbed everyone's attention, and now all eyes were looking his way. The people of Paris and the soldiers of Condé's army all stared up in awe and fear and amazement. Even though he was far away and in the dark, Greg could somehow sense Athos, surrounded by the enemy, seconds away from death. He could sense the others, too, when he thought about them: Porthos and Catherine and Louis and his parents. He held all their fates in his hand.

He looked back to Aramis, and the inscription from the crypt came back to him: *To all who would use the stone, beware. Know the difference between what you desire and what you need.*

The tempting voice in his head faded away. Those desires, Greg knew, were not his own. He didn't really care about power—and as Dinicoeur had proven, immortality was a curse, rather than a gift. That was why they called this "the Devil's Stone," because it tempted you with what was wrong. Even wanting to simply go home was a selfish desire. It didn't serve anyone but his parents and himself.

No, there was one thing he truly desired. One thing the world needed.

Paris had to be saved.

Greg unleashed the power of the stone.

There was a sudden burst of light even greater than the first. It radiated out from Greg and rocketed into the sky. All the people in Paris gazed up at it in wonder.

Then another wave of energy exploded out, only this time, Greg could control it. It blew through the city streets and knocked Condé's soldiers off their feet. It snuffed out their torches and doused the burning buildings. Their war machines collapsed. Their swords bent into useless chunks of metal. Their wonder turned to terror.

And they ran.

They ran in fear of whatever unknown power protected Paris, aware only that it was great and terrifying and that it didn't want them there. The soldiers dropped their weapons and scrambled back over the ramparts and raced back through the hole in the wall. They abandoned their camps outside the city and fled into the surrounding countryside, desperate to get as far from Paris as they could.

Within a minute, the city was free of invaders, and Condé's army was in full retreat.

Greg felt the power dissipate, as though the Devil's Stone was spent. The light dimmed until, instead of a blinding beacon, there was only the stone glowing in his hands.

Greg looked to Aramis again.

His friend was laughing, thrilled by what had happened. "I think you just saved France," he said.

NINETEEN

ARAMIS AND GREG CAREFULLY LED MILADY DOWN through the bell tower. They would have tied her hands, but there was no way for her to climb down the ladder from the roof that way, so instead they had to proceed with caution. Greg had no doubt that Milady was still plotting to get the upper hand in any way she could—and if that involved shoving them through the flimsy rail to their deaths at the bottom of the tower, she'd do it. Thus, he kept both halves of the stone safely tucked away in separate pouches and his sword trained on Milady's back. It took far longer going down than it had coming up, and by the time they reached the base, the city was already celebrating.

A great number of people had gathered in the plaza in front of the cathedral. It seemed as though half of Paris was there—and all of them wanted to know what had happened at the top of the tower. Several were relatives of Aramis, including the family members who had been so kind as to give Greg shelter after the last time he'd had a battle in the tower.

"Aramis!" they called, speaking for the crowd. "What happened up there?"

"A miracle," Aramis replied with a smile.

This seemed to be enough for most of the people, who cheered in response. Church bells began to ring in triumph all over the city, so the priests at Notre Dame realized they had better literally chime in. Soon, Emmanuel was ringing as well.

The only person who wasn't happy was Milady. Now that they were safely on the ground, Aramis got some rope and cinched her wrists behind her back. Throughout it all, she didn't say a word. She simply kept her eyes narrowed at Greg with disgust.

"Gregory!" Mom and Dad had made it out of the ancient city. They shoved through the crowd to hug their son tightly. Greg hadn't seen them so happy in months.

"D'Artagnan!" Athos came from the other direction. He'd found a piece of debris and was using it as a crutch.

He, too, gave Greg a hug, any distrust he'd ever felt long gone. "That was your doing, wasn't it?"

"Yes," Greg admitted sheepishly.

"It was incredible," Athos said. "I thought I was done for. One second, there was an enemy mob around me, ready to hack me to pieces, and the next they were all running for their lives. You should have seen the terror on their faces! I don't think they'll stop running until they get to the sea."

"So, the stone did all that?" Mom asked.

"Yes," Greg replied. "When you put the pieces together, they have far greater power than I ever imagined."

Aramis tilted his head toward Milady. "Let's get her to the palace, shall we? We can lock her up in the dungeon there."

"Plus, we need to see how the others fared." Athos looked worried as a thought came to him. "If Milady got loose, then Condé must have as well."

"Everyone is all right," Greg told them. "I could sense them all before, when I was up there. I can't explain it, but . . . Porthos, Catherine, and the king are all alive and well."

"I'm not saying I don't believe you," Aramis told Greg. "But I'd like to see that with my own eyes."

They all set off through the city. Their path took them over the Bridge of Saint Denis again and past the house where Greg had rescued his ancestors. As he stared at the still-smoking wreckage, he couldn't believe that had only happened a few hours before. This day had been the longest of his life. It felt like months had gone by. And yet he no longer felt exhausted, though he had no idea whether this was from the power of the Devil's Stone or adrenaline or the sheer joy of having succeeded in thwarting the enemy.

As they passed onto the right bank of the river, Milady brushed close to Greg. "Your friends may all be very proud of you," she whispered, "but you're a fool. All that power and you don't even know what to do with it."

Greg fixed her with a hard stare. "No," he said. "You're the one who wouldn't know what to do with it. You don't understand the stone at all."

"What do you mean?" Aramis asked.

Greg realized everyone else had heard him and was looking at him with great interest.

"It's true that the stone can give you whatever you desire, but I think that's the catch as well." He turned to Aramis. "Remember when you figured out how to translate my great-great-grandfather's diary? The last page was missing."

"How could I forget?" Aramis asked. "It was about to tell us something important about our enemies."

"'Hopefully, you will never have to confront Dominic, but if you do, there is something else you must know,'" Greg recalled. "I remember because I read that over and over again. It was so frustrating. But now I think I can guess what those pages would have said."

"What?" Mom asked.

"That Dominic's strength—his immortality—was also his weakness," Greg replied. "He thought that eternal life would be wonderful, but in truth, it was terrible for him. He was miserable for hundreds of years, and that changed him. He wasn't really Dominic Richelieu anymore. He became Michel Dinicoeur, a man full of hate and rage, a man who would actually even consider killing his own child to get even with us."

"I think you're right," Dad said. "I'm sure Dinicoeur thought that he'd simply done things wrong. That if he got another chance at immortality, he could avoid those mistakes and live happily forever. But it's very likely that no matter what happened, he would have ended up regretting his decision. As it was, all those years he spent consumed by anger and vengeance corrupted his soul. He never realized that he wasn't doing this for Richelieu; he was doing this for himself. And ultimately, it was his undoing. Michel Dinicoeur destroyed himself."

Everyone nodded agreement, except Milady, who looked annoyed at all of them. "That only proves that Dinicoeur was a fool as well."

"I don't think so," Greg said. "I think any attempt to use the power of the stone for yourself, no matter what, will end badly. They call it the Devil's Stone for a reason. It corrupts you. The only way to avoid that is to use the power for what's right."

"But what about going home?" Mom asked. "We *can* use it to get back home again, can't we? Even though that's selfish."

"I don't know if I'd consider that selfish," Aramis said. "In a sense, that's just trying to undo the damage that Dinicoeur did with the stone in the first place."

Before Greg could reply, they arrived within sight of the Louvre and heard a cheer go up. Porthos and Catherine emerged from the palace and ran to reunite with their friends.

"You did it!" Catherine cried, throwing her arms around Greg.

He hugged her back, only realizing now how worried he'd been that he might never see her again.

"Where's Condé?" Athos asked.

"We've already got him locked up in the dungeon," Porthos said. "I'm surprised you can't hear him. He's bawling like a baby." He looked to Milady and grinned. "We have a nice cold cell waiting there for you, too."

Everyone suddenly fell silent. For a moment Greg thought something else terrible might have happened, but then saw the reason for everyone's reverence: King Louis had emerged from the palace as well.

Only, he didn't quite look like himself. He wasn't done up in his usual formal clothes, nor was he flanked by his standard retinue of servants. Instead, he was still wearing his bedclothes. Two guards were tailing him. "Oh, don't stop your celebrations on my behalf," he said. "That's why I'm here. I didn't want to miss the fun."

He approached Greg, and Greg could see that something had changed in the king since he'd last seen him. Now, instead of staring dreamily at Milady, Louis avoided her as though she was a poisonous snake. "France owes you her undying thanks for your service," he said. "And *I* owe you an apology. You might have noticed that I wasn't quite myself the last time we met."

"Yes," Greg said.

"I am so sorry," Louis told him. "I don't know what came over me."

"I have a good idea," Greg said, glancing toward Milady.

Louis turned to the two guards who'd followed him. "Please take Milady here to the dungeon."

"Yes, Your Majesty," one said, though both hesitated before leaving.

"I'll be fine," Louis told them. "I'm with the Musketeers."

The guards took hold of Milady's arms and marched her into the palace. She didn't cry or beg for mercy. In fact, she didn't say a word. She just stared balefully at Greg as she walked away, as if she wanted him to know this wasn't the end for her.

Greg felt unsettled as he watched her go, but then Catherine slipped her hand into his and gave it a squeeze. "Forget about her," she said. "She won't be any trouble anymore."

Greg turned back to her and smiled. "You're right," he said. In fact, when he thought about it, with Milady and Condé locked up, Dinicoeur and Richelieu gone, and the enemy army on the run, there wasn't any trouble brewing for the first time since he'd arrived in 1615. "Let's celebrate."

"I'm all for that!" Porthos crowed, and soon the Musketeers, Greg's parents, and King Louis were all happily regaling one another with their tales of everything that had happened that night.

While Porthos and Athos gleefully tried to one-up each other in explaining how heroic they'd been, Aramis pulled Greg aside. "So," he said. "After all this time, you have the stone. Are you ready to go home?"

Greg looked around him, at the city of Paris, at the street full of revelers, at his parents, at King Louis, at Catherine and his fellow Musketeers, all full of joy and excitement.

"Not quite yet," he said. "I think it might be nice to stick around a little longer."

LE FIN

TWENTY

IN THE END, GREG AND HIS PARENTS STAYED IN PARIS FOR
two more days.

The whole time he'd been in 1615, Greg had been desperate to get home. But now that he had the opportunity,
he found he didn't want to rush his departure. The Musketeers were the best friends he'd ever had, and once he
returned to the future, he'd never see them again.

His parents understood. In fact, they were happy to stay
as well. With the king's enemies defeated, the entire city
was ready to celebrate.

Greg was surprised to realize that beyond his friends, there were other things he'd miss about life in 1615. He'd grown used to how quiet it was and how dark the sky was at night. Paris itself might have been a bit of an eyesore, but there were still some lovely spots in it, and the surrounding countryside was incredibly beautiful. But there was so much he missed about his old life—books and movies and hamburgers and ice cream and computers and flush toilets (he *really* missed flush toilets)—that he eventually knew it was time to go home.

Everyone decided that the return should take place in the throne room. After all, that was the room Greg and his family had first arrived in, and it only seemed right (not to mention properly formal) for them to leave from it as well.

Louis, the Musketeers, and Catherine gathered to see them off. Louis and Catherine wore their finest clothes, and the Musketeers wore crisp new uniforms. Greg and his parents wore the closest things they could find to modern clothing, seeing as they'd end up right out in public when they jumped back. Greg took out his phone and then handed both pieces of the Devil's Stone to Aramis.

"We'll miss you all very much," Louis told them.

"Have a good wedding," Greg said. Despite everything, Louis's marriage to Anne of Austria was still on. "I'm sorry I'll miss it."

"I'm sorry you will, too," Louis said, then asked, "It *will* work out all right, won't it?"

"Yes," Greg's father replied. "From what the history books say, you two will be a very lovely couple."

"Even though her father tried to overthrow me?" Louis asked.

"I wouldn't worry about him too much," Greg's mother said. "You just take good care of Louis the Fourteenth. He's going to do great things someday."

Greg did wonder himself if history hadn't been altered too greatly, although it did seem to be back on track. The Spanish had been repelled, Condé's army had been defeated, and life in Paris was returning to normal: The wall around the city was being mended, and all the other damage that had been done was being repaired.

"You're sure this will work?" Athos asked, looking at Greg's phone curiously. "You can actually jump back through that?"

"To be honest, I'm not quite sure," Greg admitted.

"Well then, what have we spent all this time saying good-bye for?" Porthos joked. "For all we know, you could end up stuck here forever."

"There's only one way to find out," Aramis said.

Greg nodded, then flipped on his phone. The battery was down to one percent, though that was enough for him to bring up the photo he'd taken just outside his apartment building in Queens.

"Let's do this," Dad said. "Before the power dies out."

Greg set the phone on a table, then took both pieces of

the Devil's Stone and put them together.

Once again, there was a blinding flash of light and a surge of energy that almost knocked everyone off their feet.

Greg felt the power roll through him. Then the picture on the phone rippled and became more vivid, as though it had come to life. Even though it was only an inch across, it seemed to expand somehow. It was no longer merely a photo of modern Queens. It *was* Queens. Greg could feel himself being pulled into it, back to his own time.

He shoved the stone into Aramis's hands. Over the last week, they had talked at length about what to do with it once Greg had gone home. The Musketeers would break it in two again and make sure that the two pieces could never be reunited. Porthos would ride north with one and throw it into the sea. Athos would do the same in the south. "Get rid of it," Greg said now. "Once and for all."

"I assure you we will," Aramis told him.

The time portal rippled, as though it wasn't quite stable.

Greg knew he had to go, and yet he wavered. He turned to the Musketeers, his friends, and held out his hand. "All for one . . . ," he said.

The other three placed their hands on top of his. ". . . and one for all," they chimed.

Then Greg turned to Catherine, who was wiping away tears.

"Go," she told him. "This isn't the place for you."

Greg stepped forward and embraced her. "I'll never stop

thinking about you," he said, and then kissed her.

"Hurry!" Mom said. "It's weakening!"

Sure enough, the window to the future was fading. Greg took one last look at his friends—Aramis, Porthos, Athos, and Catherine—and then turned and stepped through the portal.

His parents came with him.

A wave of energy surged through them . . . and everything changed.

The first thing that hit them was the smell. Truck exhaust and garbage and the odor of greasy fast food.

Then there was an unbelievable amount of sound: car horns, jackhammers, buses, and the hum of a thousand conversations at once.

Greg looked around him. Everything appeared exactly the same as he remembered. If anyone had noticed his family's sudden appearance on the street, they didn't show it. Greg realized he was now holding his phone. When he looked at the screen, for one last, brief moment, he could see into the past. The Musketeers were all watching him. And then the picture winked out as the phone battery died.

"We're back!" Mom cried. "Oh, Gregory, we're back!"

Greg took in his apartment building, the shops down the block, the cars whizzing by. Some of his schoolmates were playing touch football in the park across the street.

"Everything's the same." Greg sighed with relief. "Just as we left it."

"No," Dad said. "One thing's different."

"What?" Greg asked.

"*You*," Mom told him.

Greg smiled, realizing she was right. He wasn't the same timid, unskilled kid he'd been before he'd left. He was confident, brave, and chivalrous. He'd experienced adventures that most kids his age could only dream of. He was a Musketeer now, no matter what century he lived in.

"Come on," Dad said. "Let's go home."

They started up the steps to the stoop of their apartment building. As Greg climbed, he realized something *was* different. He still could still feel the power of the Devil's Stone. He'd been thinking that it was some sort of cosmic residue from the jump through time, but now he realized it was coming from somewhere on *him*.

He felt through his clothes and came upon something tucked into them.

Two things, really. Wrapped in a piece of parchment.

He unfolded the parchment and read it:

D'Artagnan—
I know you would never have agreed with this, but
I think it's best if we remove the stone from our time
altogether. Do with it as you see fit. Destroy it once and
for all—or keep it. You, of all people, can be trusted to
do the right thing with it.
—Aramis

"Greg, is something wrong?" Mom asked.

"No," Greg told her. "Everything's fine. I was just taking it all in."

He headed inside, already thinking about what to do with the stone. Perhaps he could throw one piece in the East River and ship the other to Antarctica. Or he could find a steel smelting plant and have both pieces melted.

Or he could keep them, just in case he ever wanted to visit his friends in 1615 again.

Greg smiled at the thought, then stepped into his apartment. It was good to be home.

THE ADVENTURE THAT STARTED IT ALL . . .

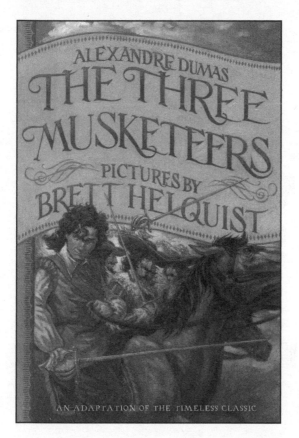

Alexandre Dumas's timeless, swashbuckling tale takes on a new life in this young readers' edition, enriched by vibrant illustrations from acclaimed and bestselling artist Brett Helquist.

Simon, driving the guard into Jean. He'd hoped to knock both of them off their feet, but since each was enormous, he merely set them off balance.

But in that moment, Aramis sprang to life. While Jean was distracted by Greg, Aramis grabbed the torch from him and turned the flame on both guards. Their shirts quickly caught fire.

The guards screamed in pain, scrambling to get their clothes off. Aramis skirted past them while Greg snatched the keys off the floor.

The other guards in the hall had now realized what was going on and moved to block Greg and Aramis's escape. But in doing so, they turned their backs on Porthos and Athos, who immediately leaped into action, taking their guards by surprise. Porthos snatched the sword from one's belt while Athos wrapped his chained wrists around the neck of the other.

That left only Catherine's guard, who charged at Greg with his sword raised. Greg parried the attack with Simon's sword while tossing the keys to Aramis, who raced to Catherine's side to unlock her chains.

For a few seconds, the narrow dungeon hall was complete chaos, with Greg, Athos, and Porthos battling the guards while Jean and Simon howled in pain and flailed about. The guards were all mere thugs, nowhere near as adept with a sword as any of the Musketeers. Greg easily disarmed his opponent and held him at sword point. Porthos did the same, while Athos knocked his opponent unconscious. Aramis unlocked Catherine's chains and then did the same for Athos.

"There," Aramis said. "You're free."

"I'm unchained," Athos corrected. "We're not free by a long shot." He turned and raced into the maze of storerooms, and the others quickly followed.

The howls of the guards they'd left in the dungeon quickly faded as the Musketeers hurried through the castle. The thick stone walls swallowed the noise. However, there were many people—cooks, maids, and other servants who'd risen early to prepare for the busy day. As the boys and Catherine ran past, they cried out with alarm.

By the time the Musketeers reached the grand banquet hall, they could hear word of their escape echoing throughout the castle.

Athos headed for the massive front doors. "Quickly!" he cried. "Maybe we can make it to the city gate before too many soldiers gather."

"No," Greg told him. "The gate's too dangerous. We're going down the cliff."

Athos spun toward him, stunned. "Down the cliff? But that's insanity."

"Which is exactly why no one will expect us to try it." Greg raced to the winch, where the sturdy rope that held up the massive chandelier was anchored.

"How on earth are we supposed to get down the wall?" Porthos asked.

"With this!" Greg hacked at the rope with his sword. It was as thick as his wrist, however, and only a few strands of it frayed.

Four guards raced into the room. Porthos fended off the first with his stolen sword, but the other Musketeers were unarmed. Athos snatched a silver candelabra off the dining table and used it to defend himself. Aramis and Catherine had no choice but to run from the third, while the fourth charged Greg. This guard was huge and armed with a spiked mace that he swung menacingly. Greg knew his sword wouldn't stand a chance against it.

He was backed up against the wall. There was nowhere to go . . . on the ground, at least. An idea of how to escape suddenly came to Greg. It was another cliché, of sorts— perhaps he'd seen way too many swashbuckling movies. But if playing dead had worked, maybe this would, too.

So he wrapped his arm around the chandelier rope and kicked out the pin that locked the winch.

The winch spun, loosening the rope, and the chandelier plummeted. The rope raced after it, spinning over the support ring in the ceiling and lifting Greg off the floor out of the path of the mace-wielding guard, who ran beneath his rising feet and crashed into the wall.

The Musketeers scrambled out of the way as the chandelier crashed onto the banquet table. The guard pursuing

Aramis wasn't quite so quick and was clobbered by the massive light fixture. Aramis grabbed the man's sword and hacked at the rope where it connected to the chandelier.

"Wait!" Greg yelled to him. His escape hadn't worked exactly as he'd hoped. In the movies, the good guy would have ridden the other end of the rope to safety. But Greg now found himself dangling high above the floor, clinging to the rope for dear life as it swung wildly about the room. If Aramis slashed the other end, he'd come crashing back down to earth.

Lord Contingnac emerged onto the mezzanine at the top of the grand staircase, roused by the commotion. "My prisoners!" he gasped, and began to race from the room, calling for more guards.

But as he did, the dangling rope whipped Greg toward him. *I can't believe I'm doing this,* Greg thought, and then let go of the rope. He sailed onto the mezzanine, slammed into Contingnac, and sent the lord flying. The rotund man crashed into a wall and tumbled to the floor. When he rolled over, Greg was looming over him, pointing the tip of his sword at Contingnac's nose.

"Call off your guards," Greg ordered. "Tell them to drop their weapons or you die."

All the lord's bravado drained from him at once. Without hesitation, he ordered, "Guards! Stand down! Drop your swords!"

In the banquet hall below, the guards obeyed. Their